*mu*
*T.ω.*

*A*
*Harlequin*
*Romance*

OTHER
*Harlequin Romances*
by DOROTHY CORK

Many of these titles are available at your local bookseller,
or through the Harlequin Reader Service.

For a free catalogue listing all available Harlequin Romances,
send your name and address to:

HARLEQUIN READER SERVICE,
M.P.O. Box 707, Niagara Falls, N.Y. 14302
Canadian address: Stratford, Ontario, Canada N5A 6W4

or use coupon at back of book.

# RED DIAMOND

by

## DOROTHY CORK

*Harlequin Books*

TORONTO • LONDON • NEW YORK • AMSTERDAM • SYDNEY • WINNIPEG

Original hard cover edition published in 1975
by Mills & Boon Limited


SBN 373-01966-1


Harlequin edition published April 1976

λ

Copyright © 1975 Dorothy Cork. All rights reserved.

Except for use in any review, the reproduction or utilization of this
work in whole or in part in any form by any electronic, mechanical
or other means, now known or hereafter invented, including xero-
graphy, photocopying and recording, or in any information storage or
retrieval system, is forbidden without the permission of the publisher.
All the characters in this book have no existence outside the imagination of the Author, and have no relation whatsoever to anyone bearing
the same name or names. They are not even distantly inspired by
any individual known or unknown to the Author, and all the incidents
are pure invention.

The Harlequin trade mark, consisting of the word HARLEQUIN and the
portrayal of a Harlequin, is registered in the United States Patent
Office and in the Canada Trade Marks Office.

Printed in Canada

# CHAPTER ONE

MARTYN, lying on her stomach on the beach behind the bungalow, took up a handful of golden sand and let it trickle slowly, slowly, through her fingers. Like an egg-timer or an hourglass or something. 'When it's all gone, Bastian and Becky will be here.'

She concentrated hard on the sand and as the last glittering grains slid away, a shadow fell and her heart leaped. She was right! Here they were! She had actually started to scramble to her feet when she discovered there was no dog, and that the man walking by her wasn't Bastian at all but a deeply tanned, rugged-looking, broad-shouldered stranger. Curiously analytic grey eyes studied her momentarily from the shadow of black eyebrows, and then, feeling slightly disconcerted, she was on her own again.

She expelled her breath gently, disappointedly, and watched this other man saunter on over the beach towards the surf, his thick black hair gleaming, the muscles of his broad brown back rippling above the dark blue swim shorts that were all he wore. Then she stretched out on the sand again to return to her vigil and her reflections. In her pale beige shorts, long white socks, and sleeveless cotton top of a deep-sea green that made her blue eyes bluer and her sun-bleached hair paler, she looked like a girl with nothing on her mind – a girl with nothing to do but lounge about in the sun at nine o'clock in the morning. But inside her head her mind was buzzing and busy.

There wasn't anyone much on the beach at this hour on a weekday, and her eyes strayed to the man who had passed by her. He had dropped his towel carelessly on the sand and was heading for the water. She was sure she had never seen him before, unless – unless he had come wading out of the sea yesterday just as she and Bastian and Becky and finished their walk along the beach. Anyhow – so what? She had other things to think about, and when Bastian came she was going to ask him to think of something to help her out. Perhaps some sort of *outdoor* job where she could use her talent for drawing, she thought, knowing even as she thought it that she was asking for the impossible. Still, at thirty-nine, more than twice her age, Bastian would surely be able to produce some ideas as to what she could do, now that Rosalind had said so very definitely that the swimming lessons were no more than a pretence at seriousness.

Rosalind had given her a week – 'One week, Bit – and I mean it,' she had warned this morning – to present her case for a reasonable and practical alternative to taking a secretarial course. If she failed, then it was off to Manly in the bus each day to learn shorthand and typewriting.

'Anything but being stuck in an office all day,' thought Martyn, laying her face down against the comforting warmth of the sand. And not having the faintest idea just what alternative Bastian was going to suggest later that morning.

Rosalind was Martyn's sister-in-law, and she had issued her edict last night.

Two months had passed since Stan had died, and that was quite long enough for Martyn to expect to be treated gently, as a sort of convalescent. Stan was Martyn's father – her brother Richard's father too, but Dick hadn't lived at home since twelve years ago when he had won a scholarship to university in Sydney and left the small coastal town where Stan Verity managed the local swimming baths. Richard had been called Dick then, and Martyn had been about seven years old – in the water more often than out of it, licking ice-cream cones between swims, running barefoot down the street to buy fish and chips for tea, her sun-bleached hair streaming, her skin white with salt, the taste of it on her lips. A waterbaby from way back who knew and wanted no other life than the one she

6

led with her father. She didn't remember her mother, who had died when she was four, and life seemed always to have been easygoing and carefree for Bit – Little Bit, as they had called her, because she was so much the baby of the family.

Then her father had died, and the whole of her life's pattern was disrupted.

Because Richard and Rosalind lived on the coast too – but in a Sydney suburb – she had thought she would transplant well enough, but she hadn't. With her deeply tanned face and body, her habit of going barefoot and of wearing the sketchiest of clothes and not caring a fig for fashion, she hadn't exactly made a hit with Rosalind, whom she had met at her wedding five years ago and seen only once since.

'Dear God, Bit, you're positively uncivilized – and not one whit older than you were at thirteen,' Ros had commented.

They had treated her like an invalid at first, because she had been so obviously flattened by her father's sudden death. Stan, Martyn had always called him. Everyone did – everyone who lived in the small town, all the kids who came swimming to the baths. He had been so husky and fit, a man who rarely wore more than a pair of shorts, sometimes adding a short-sleeved shirt with an open neck; whose body was brown and tough, whose natural background was the blue-green water of the swimming baths, or the turquoise of the Pacific Ocean. A man who, like some gnarled old tree, one somehow expected to last for ever. Never, never to have died so suddenly of a heart attack before he was sixty.

So Martyn had come south to Sydney and didn't realize till she hit the place just what a misfit she was going to be. The sea was there, of course – the same old ocean almost at the back door, but the life was completely different from the casual one she had shared with Stan way up the coast. Rosalind, and Richard, as she had learned to call her brother, lived in an attractive bungalow, furnished with good modern stuff, with airy rooms, an up-to-date kitchen and a bar. At the back, there was a tree-shaded terrace that looked across a lawn of coarse grass to the sea. Somehow Rosalind miraculously kept the floors free of the sand that blew in from the beach in white drifts across the garden. Martyn felt guilty every time she came in from the sea in case she carried sand with her. It hadn't mattered at home, but here everything was so tidy, so immaculate. Except her bedroom, though she did her best with that to the extent that it didn't seem to belong to her. No more sandshoes and swimsuits drying on the windowsill – no more shells on the dressing table.

Last evening she had come in rather late from the beach, tiptoeing, looking back to see if she had left a tell-tale trail of sand after changing on the verandah and hanging her swimsuit in the yard. Then she had gone duti-fully to the kitchen. There was a recipe card on the corner of the dresser, conspicuous under a pretty glass paper-weight, and apprehensively she had picked it up. Chicken with Cabbage. She had skimmed through the print anxiously. It looked as if she could have it ready in an hour and three-quarters at any rate. In her mind she could hear Rosalind's voice:

'If you're going to live with us, Bit, then you must make yourself useful – at least until you decide what you're going to do with your life. It might be an idea if you got the meals ready at night for a start, seeing you're idle all day.'

'But—' began Martyn hesitantly, worriedly, for she had never done much cooking.

Rosalind interrupted her. 'Now don't start telling me you can't cook. I know you've always lived on fish and prawns and pies out of a paper bag, but anyone with a little common sense can cook. You don't need to be an intellectual giant. I've got a file of foolproof recipes – you'll learn in no time.'

So last night – chicken and cabbage . . .

It was simmering gently in the heavy covered pan on

top of the stove when Rosalind and Richard came in. Martyn earned a modicum of praise and retired with a sigh of thankfulness to set the table while Richard poured the sherry.

Everything was as usual – or so it seemed. The meal was good, the other two discussed their day with each other – Ros was a radiographer, Dick was a psychology lecturer. Then they discussed a party they had been invited to, and Martyn, who had a good healthy appetite, relaxed and enjoyed her meal, and after it was over went into the kitchen to do the washing up, and protested when Rosalind came to help.

'For heaven's sake,' said her sister-in-law irritably – she was a slim imperturbable-looking girl of twenty-seven, with an air of confidence and poise that Martyn sometimes envied – 'don't act as if you're paying gratefully for your keep with humble services. That's not how we see it at all. But this is *my* home, and if it pleases me to wipe the dishes, then it doesn't require any comment. I want to talk to you, anyhow.'

Martyn's heart sank. Another talk! She bit her lip and almost dropped a plate as she lifted it into the rinsing water. She just didn't seem to fit comfortably into this household. Two months had proved it. It wasn't simply that they didn't want her, or that a third person is an intrusion between husband and wife. The fact was she didn't belong. To her, they were like people from another planet, brainy, sophisticated. She didn't understand them and they didn't understand her. Ros was out all day, but all the same, Martyn was in her hair – under her feet – far too much of the time. And she was quite sure that if *she* were Rosalind, she wouldn't want Martyn Verity around, there every night when she came home from work, there every week-end—

'How did you put in the day, Bit?' Rosalind asked after a moment of contemplatively drying the dishes.

'Oh, I gave a swimming lesson this afternoon, and I spent this morning on the beach.' She stopped short. It

9

was futile to recite it all. The swimming lessons brought in 'pocket money', Ros said scornfully, and other than that there were things that Martyn simply didn't tell them about, because they would be scorned too. About Bastian, and the drawing lessons. She knew that Ros would think of that – 'wasted time' – though she loved drawing, and Bastian said she was coming on well. At the back of her mind she had, too, an uncomfortable idea that neither Ros nor Richard would approve of Bastian, because he was older, and divorced, or for some silly illogical reason like that.

She looked through her lashes at Ros, who was frowning.

'That's fine,' Ros said vaguely, and then added briskly, 'All the same, it's time we started thinking of your future. You must have some sort of life of your own. What do you really want to do?'

Martyn could have said, 'I'd like to draw a children's picture-story book.' But she didn't, because she just knew that Rosalind would *not* say amen to that. So she said, 'There's the swimming. I could find some more pupils, answer some more ads—'

Ros's pretty eyebrows went up a notch. She commented with her usual cool control, 'I don't *really* think that's the answer, Bit. I was thinking of something that would eventually make you more or less independent. Until you get married, of course. You don't want to live here with us indefinitely, do you? I mean, it's really a more or less temporary arrangement – till you find your feet.'

'Yes, I know,' Martyn said.

'Well, then, you've had enough time to pull yourself together, and if you don't have any brilliant ideas yourself, it would seem the most sensible thing to enrol yourself at that secretarial school in Manly. With a little hard work you could be out earning your living in no time – meeting people, doing something useful, instead of frittering away your life in the water. You'd make friends –

meet some nice girls of your own age, maybe get a flat together.'

Typing. Secretarial school. To an outdoor girl, what could sound more dismal? Was it any use suggesting a course in art as an alternative? She hadn't been smart enough at school – because she hated being indoors studying had been her excuse – to get an art scholarship. And in her heart she hadn't been sorry about that, because she had loved her life exactly as it was. All she really wanted artwise, after she left school at sixteen, was the bit of tuition she had from a 'lady artist' – Mrs. Turner, who had retired up the coast with her husband. The rest of her time Martyn had spent happily in a swimsuit, helping at the baths, in the shop or the locker rooms, on the turnstiles. Smelling the sea, hearing the sound of the waves night and day, tasting salt on her lips, running round with kids her own age; looking after Stan. Of course Stan, who doted on her – Little Bit, the unexpected addition to the family – thought she was just about a genius with her drawings of seagulls and cats and dogs and kids. He was so proud of her drawings it was embarrassing. He'd have had every second one framed and put on exhibition, if wishes came true. And if it was what she had really wanted, he'd have sent her off to Sydney to live with Dick and attend some private art school no matter what it cost. Martyn had never wanted to go. 'No, thanks, Stan – life's great just the way it is. Mrs. Turner says I have the talent to do a children's book, and I don't need to go away anywhere to do *that*.'

But time went by so quickly in the sun, she'd never even got around to starting a book.

And now – secretarial school—

Richard had come to stand in the kitchen doorway and she knew they'd been making decisions. It was time for Bit to be given a push in the right direction.

'Give it a go, Bit,' her brother said encouragingly.

Martyn looked at him perplexedly. 'Not *typing*, Dick. It wouldn't – I couldn't—'

Ros cut in sharply, 'What else *can* you do, for Pete's sake? You haven't been brought up to use your brains, and let's face it, you're your father's daughter.'

Martyn's face crimsoned with hurt and anger. 'I'd have thought secretaries need brains like anyone else,' she flared. 'So—' She pulled out the plug and the water began to disappear with an enraged gurgle.

Richard said placatingly before Ros could speak, 'So they do. And no one's saying you're brainless. But the point is, if you're going to be awkward about typing, then you'd better think hard what you're going to take up instead. You know as well as we do that this just can't go on for ever.'

Even he sounded exasperated, and Martyn turned away to dry her hands on the kitchen towel. 'I'll think hard,' she told Richard. 'I promise I shall.'

'We'll give you a week,' Rosalind said. And she didn't smile . . .

So now, this morning, Martyn was waiting for Bastian – the only mature and sympathetic person she could think of who might come up with some helpful ideas. Because a week wasn't very long to make plans.

Fifteen minutes later she and Bastian and Becky, his Great Dane, were walking along the sand. This was a morning ritual. Bastian brought his dog down from the plateau for exercise, and Martyn, since the day she and Bastian had met some five or six weeks ago, always went along too. They covered almost the full length of the long beach, Bastian throwing sticks for Becky, Martyn sometimes racing along on the hard wet sand, the dog at her heels. The walk over, they would get into the car he parked in a dead end street near the bungalow and go up to his house on the plateau for coffee and for Martyn's drawing lesson. And, for Bastian, the beginning of the day's work.

Today was no different, and somehow or other they had finished their walk before Martyn said a single word about Rosalind's edict.

'You've been quiet this morning,' Bastian remarked when they had returned along the beach. He put his arm lightly around her waist and she looked up at him. He was not very tall, with grey-green eyes and crinkly light brown hair that had a touch of premature silver at the temples. Martyn thought him a rather nice man, and it seemed sad that he was divorced from his wife, Laurie. It had happened not long ago, he had told Martyn, but he had talked little of his personal life, and never about Laurie. There were two children, but they didn't talk about them either, and Martyn didn't pry. After all, her relationship with him was not really a personal one, partly she thought, because he was so much older than she was. But she imagined that behind his silence he was probably still hurt and unhappy about his broken home, and that could be one reason why he liked her company. To fill a big gap . . .

Now she said, 'Oh, I've got things to think about.'

'Such as?' He smiled down into her face.

'Such as that my sister-in-law's pushing me to change my ways,' she began. She glanced down towards the sea and saw that man with the strangely penetrating grey eyes emerging from the breakers and come striding over the sand. She turned away from him quickly and looked back at Bastian, and discovered he was frowning.

'Meeting me, do you mean? I thought you said you were keeping quiet about us – about the lessons. What does she suspect, for heaven's sake? God, I haven't even so much as laid a finger on you,' he finished, his lips twisting wryly.

Martyn coloured. 'Oh, it's nothing like *that* – it's not about you, of course. It's just they want me to learn typing or something ghastly like that. And stop – frittering away my life in the sun. I haven't told them about the drawing – they'd think it was silly. But now I'm wondering, you see, what I can do. I don't want to do typing, and they've given me a week to make up my mind.' She stopped. He had removed his arm from her waist and stooped to pick up a piece of driftwood and throw it for the dog to fetch, and when he straightened he looked at her quizzically. 'I thought *you* might have some ideas,' she told him hopefully.

'About you?' he said.

'Yes. Well, about what I could do,' she said, a little confused for some reason. 'I don't know anyone else to ask. Only you. You – you understand—'

'I'm flattered you feel that way.' They walked on a few paces, and arrived at the Veritys' back fence, half submerged in blown sand. 'We'll talk about it over coffee, shall we?'

'Later will do if you like,' she said quickly, vaguely uneasy. 'Tomorrow – I don't want to be a nuisance.'

'A nuisance?' he repeated, and she recognized something new in his tone. '*You* a nuisance?' Becky had brought back the driftwood and looked at them inquiringly. She was a young dog – Bastian had acquired her after he and his wife had parted. He continued dryly, 'Surely you must be aware that's not how I feel about you, Martyn. You're not altogether a child.'

His eyes went briefly over her body in the green top and beige shorts – to her brown thighs that contrasted so strongly with the white socks, and she looked back at him blankly. There were days – many of them – when she felt herself no more than a child. The day she had first met Bastian had been one of those days. She had been sitting on the sand, dumb and dazed and bruised, thinking of Stan, whom she would never see again – never, never, never. And she had been drawing seagulls with a desperate clumsy intensity as if by so doing she could dull her pain. Becky had come racing up and startled her, and Bastian had followed with a quick command to the dog and a reassuring, 'She won't hurt you – she's only a playful pup,' to Martyn. Then – 'What's that you're drawing?' It had been – comforting just then to have this older, mature man take a kindly interest in her drawing, and in herself. It had been almost miraculous to discover that he was an artist – and to have him offer to give her lessons, quite free ... Now he was saying, 'You're not altogether a child,' and she was far from sure that he was right. Besides, what had that got to do with being a nuisance or otherwise?

'I never begrudge a moment spent with you,' he said.

'But you've always got a load of fascinating things to do,' she protested, disturbed. 'I know I must often be just a – just a pest.'

'I don't know how you got that idea.' He paused for several seconds. 'As a matter of fact, you've been absorbing my mind utterly – utterly – for some days now.'

'Me?' They had nearly reached the car, and she couldn't quite think how this conversation had begun. 'When half the time you're so wrapped up in what you're doing you don't even know I'm there?' she said with an attempt at laughter.

'I'm always well aware of that. How could I not be? It's the law of nature,' he added with a slight smile. He opened the car door and she slid in the front while he let Becky in the back, and then he walked around the bonnet to get in the other side. Martyn felt puzzled. Bastian had never talked this way before, and she had an uncomfortable awareness of having disturbed the status quo, quite unintentionally.

Neither of them said anything as he drove away from the beach, down the main road past a few shops, then up along the winding road that led to the plateau. Up here was where she gave some of her swimming lessons, at private pools. This afternoon it would be to Tom and Nanda Fleet, and they passed the Fleets' house before Bastian reached his own garage. He lived alone in a two-storied house with a fair sized garden and a lovely view of the ocean. Martyn preceded him up the steps as she always did, he unlocked the door and let Becky run through to her bowl of water and thence, when he had opened the back door, into the yard. Martyn stopped off in the kitchen to start the coffee, and forage in the cupboard for biscuits. She had always enjoyed this little ritual, it was somehow different from doing things in Ros's kitchen, but today – today she was disturbingly conscious that once this had been – another woman's kitchen. A woman of whom she knew nothing. Laurie.

Bastian came to the door just as she had everything ready.

'Upstairs,' he directed, smiling at her – just the way he always smiled, she assured herself. Everything was perfectly all right. She loaded up the tray and carried it carefully along the short hallway and up the stairs, and no matter how much she reassured herself, deep down she had this feeling that somehow she had started an avalanche falling.

Upstairs there were three bedrooms, a bathroom and a shower room, and upstairs again there was a big room like an attic. Bastian had had this house especially built for him, and the attic, which had a wide window that looked from the plateau over houses and gum trees towards the ocean, was his studio. He worked for a correspondence art school, correcting lessons, and in his free time he did some easel painting. Martyn was always fascinated to see what his correspondence students had produced. Some of them were skilled and some were clumsy, but Bastian gave the same serious conscientious treatment to them all.

This morning as she poured the coffee and passed the biscuits, he opened his post as usual. He had put on his glasses which made him look businesslike and quite a bit older, and was slitting open packets and glancing quickly at one or two drawings. Martyn thought with a feeling that vacillated between relief and puzzlement that he had forgotten her quandary, and her appeal for his help. On a small easel at one side of the room was a portrait he was painting in oils of Martyn, and she studied it thoughtfully while he was occupied. A girl with rather round blank blue eyes, straw-coloured hair, a brown face and a string of coral around her neck. As a matter of fact, she looked as if she were wearing nothing but that string of coral,

16

and there was something in the expression portrayed by mouth and eyes that made Martyn feel slightly uncomfortable. It just wasn't really her.

She finished her coffee and felt sure now he had forgotten her problem completely, until with a positive action he pushed his papers aside and looked at her over his dark-rimmed glasses.

'Do you want to draw this morning? Or are we going to deal with this problem of yours?'

Martyn looked at him helplessly, no longer sure she should have asked his advice. She said, stammering a little, 'It – it doesn't matter. I don't – I don't really expect there's anything much you can suggest. I mean, it's not as if I were good enough at art to do anything – I shouldn't have asked.'

He took his glasses off and his grey-green eyes met hers. 'Don't panic. Of course there's something I can suggest, and it's perfectly simple. You don't have to run away and learn typing. I'd like you to – belong to me.'

He smiled faintly as he said it, and Martyn stared uncomprehendingly. Her mind seemed to have gone quite blank with pure astonishment. Her mouth fell open, but she was incapable of uttering a sound. He was telling her – he was telling her he was in love with her! And she had never even suspected it. Not for a single moment.

He said wryly, 'Is it really so surprising? Surely you're aware that you're very very pretty, and very very desirable.' He spared a glance for the portrait and then his eyes returned to her.

'But,' said Martyn, her head whirling, 'you've never – you've never even kissed me.'

'I've wanted to,' he said. 'It's been a – noble deference to your rather tender years. And perversely, I've even enjoyed the exquisite torture. To have you here, to look at you, and not to touch . . . Well, what do you say? That you'd prefer the typing?'

Martyn shook her head bewilderedly. If this was a proposal, then it was an unconventional one, to say the least.

But then Bastian was an artist, and as well, he'd been married before. As for whether or not she was in love with him, it was such a completely new idea that she just didn't know. She said, 'I don't know. I've just – I've just never thought about getting married, not for ages. I'm not – I'm not old enough.'

He raised his eyebrows. 'I wouldn't worry about that,' he said, not very explicitly, after a moment. 'The point is do you like me enough to consider it? If you want some time to think it over, then of course you may have it, but I'd rather gathered the matter was urgent in your young life. Was I wrong?'

'No,' she said helplessly. She hadn't even the vaguest idea what she felt about him. Could she be in love with him? Was that why she had enjoyed her mornings with him so much? Was it even, perhaps, why she had kept it all a secret? The fact was, she didn't know even the first thing about love, and so far he hadn't taught it to her. Out of deference for her tender years! She looked at him almost shyly, trying to see him anew. His narrow face, his long grey-green eyes, his light brown kinky hair. Suddenly none of it was familiar any more. It was like looking at a stranger. And odder still, superimposed on his image was that of another man – heavily built, darkly tanned, positive. Where on earth had she seen *him*? Down on the beach this morning, of course. She blinked the image away impatiently.

Bastian reached across the table and took her hand, his thumb stroking her palm. 'You're sitting there looking so stunned. Are you shocked? Aren't you interested? Would you rather forget it?'

Martyn swallowed. It all seemed so unreal. Bastian in love with her! Girls were always supposed to be flattered when someone wanted to marry them, but she couldn't take it in. It was as if she had given herself an extra problem in turning to him for help. She withdrew her hand from his and from the unnerving tickling of his thumb. 'I'll have to think about it,' she said huskily.

'Do that,' he agreed. 'I can see I've turned today really upside down for you. We won't have a lesson. I don't think either of us could concentrate. You run off home and think it over, and tomorrow we'll talk again, and lay a few more of our cards on the table.'

He smiled at her and she smiled back, feeling relieved, even reprieved. She gathered up the cups and put them on the tray just as she always did, he put on his glasses, and she went downstairs to the kitchen.

While she was rinsing the cups, she tried to remember exactly what he had said. Had he said he loved her? He had asked her, she thought, if she loved him enough to 'consider' it – not simply if she loved him. It was – odd. The trouble was, he was so experienced, and she was so horribly *in*experienced.

She tidied the cups away, and looked around the kitchen, clean and shining and neat with its breakfast nook, where once Laurie and the two nameless children had sat with its coffee percolator, and pop-up toaster, its big gleaming two-door fridge and the latest in electric stoves. Everything always looked nice and clean and she knew that a housekeeper came in three times a week to keep it so. Why had his marriage broken up? What had gone wrong between him and Laurie? Marriage, she reflected soberly, was a pretty serious business.

Feeling unaccustomedly nervous, she went to the foot of the stairs to call out, 'I'm going, Bastian. I'll see you tomorrow.'

She supposed he answered, but she didn't hear him, and of course he was already immersed in his work. Rather meditatively, she wished he had kissed her. It might have made all the difference. She might have known then how she felt about him. And he had said that *not* kissing her had been exquisite torture.

Suddenly, now she was on her own, it all seemed exciting, thrilling, but she knew she wasn't going to be able to talk to Ros and Dick about it. She would have to do all her thinking for herself . . .

In the afternoon, she went back up to the plateau to give her swimming lesson at the Fleets'. Tom and Nanda had been her first pupils and their lessons were nearly ended now. They had both become quite confident in the water, but all the same Martyn gave them her full attention that afternoon, and refused to think about Bastian. It was a bad thing to be preoccupied when you were dealing with small children and water.

Mrs. Fleet had not put in an appearance at all today, and it was only when the lesson was over that she became aware of someone watching her from beyond the shimmering blue water of the small pool. She looked across the garden as the two children scrambled on to the black and white tiles that divided the pool from the lawn, and then she blinked hard. She must be seeing things! But she wasn't. Most definitely, it was that powerful-looking, deeply tanned man she had seen this morning on the beach. Standing in the feathery shade of some wattle trees, smoking, and looking at her in such a speculatively intent way that suddenly as never before she was conscious of herself in her simple black one-piece swimsuit. Conscious of her long brown legs and tanned face, of the silver-straw hair that, stiff with salt, fell against her cheek and over her shoulders. And she remembered, strangely, that Bastian had said she was pretty – and desirable.

The children were racing for the house, for lemonade and chocolate biscuits and goodness knows what, and in a moment Martyn would follow them. Not for lemonade and biscuits, but for the clothes she had left in the bathroom, and for the money she would be paid for the lesson. And to report to Mrs. Fleet on Tom's and Nanda's progress. She had to pass by the man who was watching her on her way to the house, and she felt oddly defensive. Surely he must remember seeing her this morning – and yet there wasn't even the glimmer of a smile on his face. On the contrary, he continued to regard her through half-closed, glittery eyes, in a way that, taken in conjunction with the cynical set of his mouth, suggested there was something decidedly unlikeable, or maybe worse, about her.

'What's biting *you*?' she asked silently, as she came towards him. But all she said was a careless 'Hi!' when she was really close.

His heavy eyebrows slanted and he took the cigarette from his lips but didn't return her greeting. Nor did he remark, as she had somehow suspected that he might, that he had seen her at the surf earlier in the day. Instead he told her with a cold indifference, 'When you're ready, I'll drive you home.'

Mrs. Fleet always insisted on doing that, and she looked at him questioningly, disturbed by something in his attitude. It wasn't just his offhandedness that bothered her. It was something else entirely, something that she couldn't analyse. From this close, she saw he was far from being a conventionally good-looking man. In fact, she didn't think you could call him good-looking at all. She guessed he must be round about Bastian's age, though it was hard to tell with someone as big and muscular and assured as he was. But his eyes – she thought they were the hardest eyes she had ever seen in her life. They were like grey steel, yet they had a curious brilliance. Diamonds, she thought. Smoky diamonds. It was not till later that she knew how apt her thought had been. The thick waving black hair she had noticed earlier in the day was ruffled now, but so shiny she knew he had washed the salt from it, and his tan looked darker still against the bronze and viridian of the classy shirt he wore, open almost to the waist, revealing a dark hairy chest.

She took in everything about him with extraordinary speed while he spoke to her, and then, as a kind of retaliation to his unfriendliness, she said, cool too, 'You don't need to bother driving me. I can walk – or take the bus.'

He shrugged his too-broad shoulders carelessly, and told her, 'I'll be ready when you are. Don't rush it. There's a glass of lemonade for you on the verandah.'

Martyn blinked her blue eyes, hesitated for the fraction of a second, then moved on. Some city people – not Bastian! – could be so distant and unfriendly and patronizing. Though *he* didn't look exactly a typical city-dweller! He didn't accompany her to the verandah, but stayed where he was, and she poured lemonade from the bottle into the single glass that stood on the tray and drank it standing, her mind alert. She could hear the children romping and squealing somewhere inside the house, and a woman's voice speaking to them, but their mother didn't appear. She wondered about the matter of her pay as she set down her empty glass and headed for the bathroom where she had shed her clothes. She needed the money – if only to justify herself to Rosalind, to prove that she was earning something. Or didn't that matter any more? If she decided to marry Bastian—

In the bathroom she got out of the black cotton swimsuit, put on panties and bra, her beige shorts and the green top – her long socks and canvas shoes. She met her own blue gaze squarely in the mirror and thought with utter amazement, 'Someone wants to marry me!' What would Stan have thought? What would he have advised? Quick tears sprang to her eyes and she dashed them away. She could imagine Stan's frown – his surprise—

The dark-haired man was waiting for her on the verandah when she came out, and she found herself going over his points. He would make a good swimmer. He was broad-chested, muscular, a little over Stan's height – maybe an inch under six feet, she judged, not all that tall. But tough-looking. Tougher than anyone she had ever met. She didn't think she liked him much, he was too forbidding. Maybe he found girls as young as she was a bore, or else he had a down on modern youth.

'Ready?' he said, as she appeared, and those adamantine eyes passed over her as impersonally, now, as the beam of a torch. *Didn't* he remember her? Not even now she had on the same gear she had worn on the beach? She was sure he must, but he was too lordly, too high and mighty, to acknowledge it. Well, who cared?

She said firmly, 'No, I'm not quite ready. I have some money to collect.'

'That's right.' One hand, broad, brown, powerful-looking, went to his shirt pocket, and he added mockingly, 'I've got your pay packet here.'

'Martyn – Martyn Verity,' she supplied, thinking he had paused for her name. But she was wrong, because he didn't repeat either part of it, but handed her an envelope which she tucked away quickly in her beach bag. 'Thanks.'

He followed her down the steps and told her back, 'If you're wondering, my sister had to go out. Hence the delegation of duty.'

His sister. So Mrs. Fleet was his sister. Well, that was the first bit of information he had offered. She supposed it would be too much to expect him to introduce himself.

'How far do we have to go?' he asked as he opened the car door for her a minute later.

'Only down to the beach,' she said, and added pertly, 'Near where you saw me on the sand this morning. Remember?'

He waited till he'd got into the car beside her, slammed the door shut and started up the motor before he said, with a swift appraising flick of his eyes that seemed to take her all in anew, 'Sure I remember.' He added gratuitously and disagreeably, 'You know, I wonder about kids like you. You flit around older men like moths around a flame, playing with something you don't know a thing about. God knows how many of you get burned – and burned badly. You now – obviously green, indecently, horribly young – haven't you a family who cares what you get up to, who you kick around with?'

Her blood had frozen at his tone, and she felt herself immediately on the defensive. What sort of a mind did he have – after merely seeing her walking on the beach with a perfectly respectable man, and a dog? Possibly he had seen Bastian put his arm around her waist, but so what?

She told him icily and with a feeling of slight triumph, just to take him down a peg or two, 'As it happens that – *older* man I'm *experimenting* with wants me to marry him.'

'Good God!' The car swerved slightly as he took the last wide turn down from the plateau, and then he braked before swinging into the main stream of traffic. 'You can't mean it! You're no more than a school kid. Are you sure it's marriage he wants? And what do your parents have to say? I wonder they even let you associate with Bastian Sinclair. Or don't they know?'

She was taken aback to discover he knew Bastian's name, and said with heightened colour, 'If you know Bastian, then I can't think what you're going on about.'

'Can't you?' he grated. 'Well, I don't know him personally. I'm sure he's very charming, but I've heard quite enough about him and his affairs from my sister to know he's not a man I'd have allowed either of my younger sisters to run around with.'

'Really?' Martyn was shaking inwardly. 'Well, I *do* know him personally, and you have no right to talk like that about anyone you don't know. It's – it's unforgivable, and I'm not in the least interested in your nasty second-hand opinions. I don't want to hear any more of them, thank you. This is my street,' she added haughtily, glancing from the car window.

He swung the wheel and with tyres squealing they were round the corner, and in seconds he had pulled up at the end of the street facing the beach and turned in his seat to face her grimly.

'I've a good mind to go right into that bungalow and have a word with your mother. Someone should give you a down-to-earth talking to.'

Martyn's skin prickled with anger. 'Go ahead. But there's no one at home. I'm staying with my brother and his wife, anyhow, and they're both at work.' She reached

24

for the door-handle and struggled with it for a second till he leaned across, and putting steel-hard fingers round her wrist dragged her hand away.

'Just hang on. So there's no one I can tell tales to. Well, you're not getting out yet. I'm going to do some talking. Come on now, are you actually considering marrying this man? And are you sure it's marriage he's after? Frankly, I hope to God you're shortly going back home to your parents and school and safety, and a decently supervised life.'

She jerked her hand away from beneath his. 'I'm nineteen. I don't go to school. And my parents – I don't have any. My father died a little while ago—' Her voice broke slightly and she turned away. 'Now let me out of here—'

It was a useless plea. 'So you're in your brother's care,' he pursued remorselessly. 'And does *he* know about this idiotic affair?'

'My friendships are my own concern,' she said angrily. 'I don't have to tell Richard about everything I do and everyone I know.'

'At *your* age? And in your obvious – well, one would *presume* obvious – state of unsophistication? And when you're babbling about marriage, or most likely some state far less permanent? What utter drivel!' Those hard eyes bored into her. 'You make a full confession to your brother – I don't want to hear it – and listen hard to what he tells you. Bring your boy-friend along to meet the family before you rush into marriage or any other arrangement. My own advice would be to forget all about Sinclair as from right now. Your heart won't break, I promise you that. Young hearts are very pliant. You'll do yourself irreparable damage if you're besotted enough to get seriously mixed up with him. You're a good-looking kid – there are plenty more romances ahead of you.'

Martyn opened her mouth to utter some sort of protest, but he went on relentlessly, 'You tell this man no, you

25

hear me? He has no right to ask *anything* of a girl like you. Get out while you're still in one piece. Don't fool yourself that a kiss is just a kiss, either. After the kiss there's a further step, and then another, and before you know what's happened, you've been eased all the way from the patio or the beach or wherever right through the bedroom door ... Does he come to the bungalow when you're here alone?'

Martyn said tightly, her cheeks crimson, and not caring in the least what interpretation he put on what she said, because he was so hateful it was just humiliating – and she was hurt, hurt right through at being treated to this by an absolute stranger – 'No! I go to *his* house up on the plateau. We're alone *there*.'

A nerve twitched on his jawline. 'Good God! And it hasn't happened yet?'

'*What* hasn't happened yet?' she asked furiously.

He closed his eyes for a second. 'Are you equivocating? Or don't you know anything at all about your – would-be lover?'

She waited for a moment for self-control. 'If you mean he's divorced – yes, I know all about that.'

'All?' he quizzed.

'What do you mean?'

'If you knew it all, you just mightn't be so damned complacent. Though I don't know – you just could be more depraved than seems possible, from those desperately young heaven-blue eyes.'

She reached for the door and again he had her by the wrist.

'Let go,' she commanded. 'You're hurting me.' She added fiercely, 'Bastian is perfectly nice – he's never—'

He had released her instantly but without apology. 'Perfectly nice!' he mocked. 'Despite a reputation that states the opposite? I know something about that, I assure you, though I only visit the coast once or twice a year.'

Martyn looked back at him wide-eyed, scornful, heart thumping. 'Reputation? What do you mean?'

'With women, of course. That was what the divorce was all about. Not one woman, but—' He stopped. 'Yet he had a decent wife, a couple of nice children.'

Her cheeks crimsoned, her head was spinning. She knew nothing about the divorce. She hadn't even, when she came to consider it, the faintest idea whether or not there were other women in Bastian's life – beside herself. She saw him in the mornings. What he did with his evenings, his week-ends, she wouldn't have a clue. The truth was it had never bothered her. And now she wished she had never mentioned Bastian to this man, whoever he was. Julia Fleet's brother.

She said with an attempt at dignity, 'I don't listen to gossip.'

'Very virtuous of you,' he snapped back. 'But you'd have to have the charms of a siren to turn him into a faithful husband – or a faithful lover – overnight. And while I'll allow you're attractive – your eyes are devastating, your figure likewise – in worldly experience I'd say you were at a very heavy disadvantage.'

Martyn turned her eyes away from him. 'Will you please let me get out of this car?'

'Certainly. But I hope you'll think about what I said. Though I suppose you'll go ahead and do what you damned well please and ruin your life, if that's how you feel. You kids just won't believe you're asking for trouble when you pick up with an older man. Until hard experience brings it home to you—'

'Bastian's no older than you,' Martyn retorted determinedly.

'So what's that to do with it? Believe me, I could twist you *right* around my little finger if I had a mind to it. You just wouldn't have a clue what was happening to you. But I don't happen to have a taste for corrupting waterbabies,' he concluded disparagingly.

Martyn bit her lip and wished she could think of something utterly killing and obliterating to say. But she couldn't, so she opened the door and slithered out.

27

'Thanks for all the free advice – Methuselah,' was the best she could manage. 'But I can handle my life without your interference.'

'Then you must be a lot sharper than you look – or act,' he shot back. He slammed the door shut and drove off without even bothering to say good-bye.

# CHAPTER TWO

To her intense annoyance, as she went inside Martyn found she couldn't stop thinking about that man and all the things he had said to her – hurled at her! Everything was confused. *Did* Bastian have a reputation with women? More important still, *had* he asked her to marry him? She had, she supposed, taken it for granted, but now, rack her brains as she might, she couldn't remember that he had put it in plain words. So what had he meant? Did he just want her to go and live with him? Did he think she was that sort of girl? It was unbelievable. They had got on so well together, had such happy mornings on the beach and in his studio. And all the time he had been wanting to kiss her but not doing it. Uneasily she recalled occasions when she had caught him looking at her in a funny sort of way. She had thought it had been an artist's way – that he had been seeing her as a subject rather than as a person.

Oh, that man had spoiled everything, she thought frustratedly. Tomorrow she would see Bastian again and she'd discover that everything was as ordinary and straightforward as she had believed before. The only problem was to decide if she was even a little in love with him. She wished and wished that Ros hadn't pushed her into so tight a corner . . .

She hung her swimsuit in the garden, determinedly discarded her troubled thoughts and went into the kitchen to discover what culinary feat she had to perform tonight. There were still the ordinary tasks of everyday life to be done, thank goodness.

Lamb cutlets with pineapple rings, the recipe was headed. And presently, in the midst of patting crumbs on to the cutlets with a knife, she stopped to reflect with a faint smile – 'Love and lamb cutlets!' Yet she hadn't, when she came to consider it, been thinking of Bastian –

she'd been thinking of a few things she'd like to say to that man, for putting horrible thoughts and suspicions into her mind.

She was slicing the rough outside from a big fresh pineapple on a chopping board when another irrelevant thought surfaced. *He* had said he only came here once or twice a year. So where was he from? And would he still be at the Fleets' next time she went to give a lesson? She hoped *not*. Because if he was, she was going to ignore him. Completely. And if he asked any interfering personal questions, she would tell him quite plainly to mind his own business . . .

The following morning, feeling unaccustomedly nervous she went out to meet Bastian as usual. As she crossed the garden, she noticed she hadn't brought in her swimsuit. Last night Rosalind had said impatiently, 'Bit, please don't leave your bathing things draped around the garden. You make the place look like a – like a slum, or a laundry.'

'I'm sorry,' she had said automatically.

Well, her bathers could stay there till later on, so long as she brought them in before Ros came home . . . She climbed the low fence and plodded across the dry sand, barefooted, her sandals in her hand. Bastian must be there already, because Becky came bounding up from nowhere, to put her big paws up on Martyn's chest, and nearly knock her over as she tried to lick her face. Then Bastian appeared, and they took their walk as usual. He didn't refer to what had been said yesterday, and they threw sticks for Becky, and Martyn raced along the hard wet sand with the dog just as if nothing had happened.

But later she caught herself looking covertly at the man with whom she walked, trying to find out – *something* about him. What Stan would have thought of him, perhaps whether she was in love with him a little – or more than a little – or not at all; and – yes, if he looked like a man with a reputation with women.

It was annoying to be bugged by such thoughts, and that man was to blame. He was to blame too for her nagging suspicion that it had not been marriage Bastian had been proposing to her yesterday.

Her glance had strayed away to the prancing dog, and then to the sea. And to a lone swimmer, away out beyond the breakers. *That man* – she was positive it was he. 'Spying on me – on *us*,' she thought, as Bastian put his arm casually around her waist so that she was conscious of the touch of his slim artistic fingers through the thin stuff of her shirt. Disconcertingly, she wanted to pull away, but with a deliberate effort of will, she didn't.

A quarter of an hour later they were in his house. He went upstairs while she made the coffee, and the kitchen seemed strange today. She listened in the hallway and when there were no sounds from above, she went into the sitting room. Looking for what, she didn't know. She already know there were no photographs there, nothing to show what Laurie and the children had been like. This morning, she could smell carnations very faintly, though there were no carnations to be seen. So – another woman? Last night? Suddenly she hated herself. She was developing a suspicious mind rather quickly, wasn't she?

She went quickly and silently back to the kitchen and took the tray upstairs. Bastian was already at work on some of his correspondence lessons – as though he had something to catch up? – and he drank his coffee abstractedly. Martyn, when she had finished hers, did some drawings from sketches she had made a couple of days earlier. They were just about the worst drawings she had ever done, and when, a little later, Bastian interrupted his work to take a look at them, he finally removed his glasses and said with a faint smile, 'Hopeless! Your mind's not on it. I think I'm going to have to excuse you today. And while mid-morning's not generally considered the best time for talking of love – or making it – we more or less promised each other yesterday, didn't we? Unless you've decided in the meantime to give me the brush-off. And I don't think you have, have you?'

He looked at her steadily and she coloured and swallowed, feeling her mouth go dry.

'No,' she said uncertainly, and without really knowing what she was doing she stood up and reached for the tray.

He came round the table swiftly. 'Forget the cups, Martyn. Now we've started on this we'd better have it right out. I can't wait a week.' His hands moved to her elbows, anchoring her arms against her sides. He was very close to her, his eyes on her lips, and she felt her heart begin to hammer. Then with a deft and unexpected movement he had her locked hard in his arms and she was being kissed – horribly, savagely, as if he were going to devour her.

Perhaps three seconds passed before she summoned the strength to push him away, and she did so violently, her elbows against his chest. She had strong arms – she hadn't done all that swimming for nothing – and it wasn't so hard. But she was shaking, and she felt sick – sick – and outraged. She knew now, without any doubt, that her answer to any proposition Bastian might make would be, just as that unlikeable man had insisted, a very loud No. If being kissed by a man is so distasteful, then how could you possibly put up with any further intimacies?

Her mind went with a kind of compulsion to the couch that stood against one wall of the attic. A narrow couch where she had sat while he did studies of her for the portrait he had since painted. The bedrooms were downstairs – and she couldn't by any stretch of the imagination see herself being eased down there.

Neither of them had spoken since she pushed herself free of him, and she could see his chest rising and falling. He was breathing hard and his eyes looked dark, the pupils enlarged. He said with a crooked smile, 'I do believe you've just had your first lesson in love, Martyn. I'm sorry. It's a surprise to find anyone quite so pure. Don't be shocked – I was just a bit carried away. I'll be gentler next time, I promise.'

Next time? There wasn't going to be a next time, and she had to tell him so. She had been kissed before, of course – by boys she had known up the north coast. But they had been *boys*. His way of kissing – it was quite new to her and it was – horrible, horrible.

She said with an effort, knowing her face had whitened under its tan, that perspiration had broken out on her forehead and upper lip, 'I'm sorry, I don't think I could—' She stopped and shook her head and turned away from his eyes that were watching her so closely.

'I've frightened you,' he said. 'I've spoilt it all, have I? I rather wondered about that. But the only way to find out is to try it. So where do we stand now? If I promise, most faithfully, to teach you more gently in future, do you feel you could move in with me? Or does the secretarial course seem preferable now?'

Martyn forced herself to look at him. He didn't want her to marry him – he had never asked her. That hateful man had been hatefully right. She said a little pathetically, 'You don't want to marry me, do you?'

He didn't answer for a moment, then he said deliberately, 'I was going to talk to you about that. If you remember, I said we'd lay our cards on the table. I see it this way – and I speak from personal experience. Marriage is a business arrangement. Love is – love. Love is an art. Love is something to be enjoyed. Young people these days recognize and admit this. So – no. I'm certainly not ready to talk about marriage yet. Not when I haven't even made love to you. You're young. You don't want to tie yourself up with anyone yet. If you moved in with me, you'd be quite free – that's a promise. I'm honestly trying to help you out, Martyn, to help you to independence and the way of life that suits you. You're hamstrung while you're living with people who want to dictate to you. Free yourself – act grown-up – make the break.'

Martyn listened, completely unconvinced. *This* was

not the way to make the break. And she wasn't one of the young people who saw marriage as a business arrangement. Marriage meant love too, and as well it was an old tradition. If it needed effort to make it work, then the very effort had its own value. She knew this instinctively and very positively, so she told Bastian what that man had told her to say. She said simply and unequivocally, 'No.'

His look changed to one of frowning impatience. 'So the whole thing's to be over, is it? Just because of one kiss. I suppose you won't trust me now – won't want to come here again, or even meet me on the beach.'

'I think it would be better,' she said stiffly, knowing he would think her prudish.

'So it's off to the typewriter for you, is it?' he said with faint contempt. 'I'd have expected more character from you, Martyn. It's a shame about the drawing. You were a good pupil with a lot of talent. I'd have liked to see it develop.'

He paused and she stood with eyes downcast. She had never felt so gauche, so much at a loss. It seemed a crazy thing to have happened, and it had happened so suddenly. She had *liked* him – she had been so happy about their relationship. And now it was ending like this – vanishing as completely as a soap bubble.

She heard him sigh, and looked up, and when he spoke again his voice had lost its derision, its contempt.

'You're not feeling at all grateful to me just now, are you? But one day you may look back and decide I wasn't altogether a villain. It's been a very great temptation having a beautiful young girl like you captive in my attic week after week ... Well, go in peace.' He flung out his long-fingered hands. 'Perhaps you're right. It wouldn't work. For me it would be too close to fantasy. For you – to sordid reality. You want to dream a little longer.' He looked at her long and levelly. 'Good-bye, Martyn.'

He turned abruptly and went back to his work, and she bit her lip. When she said, 'Good-bye, Bastian,' the words

34

were scarcely audible. She had a feeling of anticlimax — and of unreality. The curtain had come down on a play that had been a lamentable failure. Bastian didn't look up, so she took the tray downstairs, and though she had intended to dump it in the kitchen and disappear as fast as she could — to run, because she felt like running — she didn't. She washed up, wiped out the sink, put everything tidily away. And then, just as on any other day, she went to the foot of the stairs and called out, 'I'm going, Bastian.' But this time, instead of adding, 'I'll see you tomorrow,' she called a clear and final, 'Good-bye'.

He didn't answer. And that was that.

She walked slowly back home from the plateau, and thought about love and about being young, and about acting grown-up and freeing herself, as Bastian had said. But this was no way to go about it. Stan would have told her that. Sooner secretarial school than playing such dangerous games with something as important as love. When it came to love, she had always kept right in the shallows. She'd paddled, innocently. She'd never struck out from the shore into the deep waters. Oh, she knew plenty about love — theoretically. She'd listened to girls talking, she'd been to films, read books, had schoolgirl crushes and other crushes that were a little more real. She hadn't been wrapped in cotton wool; she hadn't buried her head in the sand. The thing was, she had never wanted to hand over her body to anyone. Stan had told her long ago, 'You respect your body, Bit, and other people will respect it too. That way, you need never be afraid of sex or of love.' It was a kindly if rough-and-ready way of giving her a little of the instruction that perhaps her mother would have given her, and it was something she had always believed in and hung on to.

With Bastian, she reflected, as she walked down the long hill in the hot sunshine, she had honestly thought she had an uncomplicated and totally platonic friendship. Without actually putting it into words even in her

35

thoughts, she had seen him as a sort of older cousin, or a rather young uncle. That kind of thing. Safe, and to be trusted. Sex had never come into it – yet it had been there in his mind all the time. And she had made it so easy for him to bring it out into the open. Now everything was spoilt. But *not* because she had played around with an older man, and irrationally she hated that man who had preached to her and whose advice she had so quickly and unintentionally taken. She wished now she had never let him in on her private life.

Back at the bungalow she made herself a sandwich, drank a glass of milk, then got into her bathing gear. Not the black cotton, but a pert green swimsuit she had acquired since coming to Sydney – a present from Dick. She hopped over the back fence and went across the sand towards the surf. She felt disturbed and shaken up, and the sound of the sea was soothing. The beach was almost deserted and she spread out her towel and lay face down on it, soaking up the hot, hot sun, determined to keep her mind a blank. She was back with her predicament, and she could see only one end to it – Martyn Verity, typist. So she wasn't going to think about it. Not now.

She fell asleep in the sun, and she didn't know how much later it was when she awoke. *Something* had wakened her, and she sat up and stared around her and blinked hard.

There, not twenty feet away, was that man. His back was towards her, but she recognized him instantly as he stood there, his muscular torso gleaming bronze against the turquoise sea.

She sat quite still, hugging her knees and watching him, as if bemused. After a few seconds he tossed down his towel and ran down to the surf, the muscles of his back rippling. He waded into the water amongst the few other surfers, dived under a towering wave, and surfaced beyond the rush of white surging foam. Then with a powerful stroke he began to swim out. What a swimmer he was! Despite herself, she was impressed, and illogically irritated.

Without really thinking what she was doing, she re-fastened the clip that held her blonde hair back from her face, got up and kicked some sand over her towel so it wouldn't blow away, and went into the sea. Soon she too was swimming out beyond the waves, her hair, darkened by the water, sleek against her head, her eyelashes glittering points, the sun striking spangles of light from the sea around her.

Waterbaby? She could handle the ocean as well as he could!

Well out beyond the line of breakers, she paused to look around and locate him. He was swimming away from her, parallel with the shore, and Martyn took a breath, put her head down, and began to chase him, swimming as fast as she knew how. He was a powerful swimmer with a good clean style, but she thought she could catch him up. What her purpose was, she didn't stop to think, but there was some vague idea at the back of her mind about 'showing him'.

She was within fifteen feet of him when he stopped swimming, trod water, and turned in her direction. Martyn kept her head down, put on a spurt, and glided past him. Then she too trod water and swivelled round, blinking the sea from her eyes and staring as if it had just struck her who he was.

'Hi!'

He tossed the thick hair back from his forehead, and those strange grey eyes reached for her across the dazzling water, cynically informing her that she couldn't fool him. Her little act was just too amateurish for a man who could, if he wanted, twist her round his little finger.

'Well, it's the waterbaby,' he marvelled, making no attempt to remember her name. 'Or should I say mermaid, seeing you're well out of a mere waterbaby's depth? Is our meeting just a happy coincidence, or have you possibly been chasing me?'

Martyn drew a hand across her eyes, partly to dash

away the salt water, partly to hide her red face. She said shortly, 'What do *you* think?' and tried to imply by her expression that he was flattering himself if he thought she was chasing *him*.

He looked back at her mockingly. 'I think you've been chasing me. So what do you want?' His eyes were bright and hard in the sunlight. 'To tell me I was right the other day? That you've taken my advice and broken it off with your Lothario? Let's have it quickly. I'm not interested in floundering about here. In thirty seconds I'm swimming back to the shore.'

'You can go now if you like,' Martyn retorted. 'I'm not interested in taking your advice, past, present or future. It just would seem a shame the ocean isn't bigger, wouldn't it? Then we wouldn't have bumped into each other.' She did a quick turtle dive, and was soon riding a wave in to the shore and pretending to herself that she didn't feel snubbed. She had tumbled to her feet in the shallow water and was about to trudge out on to the sand when he arrived on the next wave, almost at her feet. She waited till he too was upright, and when he made to walk past her she asked aggravatingly, 'What's biting you? Why are you so scared of me? Are you married or something?'

He faced her, hands on his hips, his dark chest glistening with water. 'I'm not scared of you. I'm not married. I'm not divorced either. Any more questions? No? Right, then get this straight — when I suggested you should forget your Don Juan I wasn't suggesting you should attach yourself to me. Understand?'

'Don't worry, I wouldn't think of it.' Martyn was no longer smiling and bright. She was seething and more put out than ever. Why on earth hadn't she stayed in the sun on the sand, where she was warm and comfortable and at peace? She couldn't think what incomprehensible impulse had made her go racing off into the sea thinking she could make an impression with her swimming. But she wasn't going to step down, and as he left the water she walked along near him. She said bitingly, 'I suppose even if you're not married, an older man like you might be embarrassed to have a kid like me tramping along at your side like a moth flitting around a flame.'

'Not at all.' His mouth, which was wide with a rather full lower lip, curved slightly. 'I've lived too long to be embarrassed by a little thing like that, mermaid—'

'My name's Martyn,' she reminded him coldly. 'Martyn Verity.'

He shrugged as if he couldn't have cared less. 'Go find someone else to play with – preferably your own age. I'm not interested.' He had reached the place where he'd left his towel, stooped for it, mopped up his face, tossed it down again and took up his shirt instead – a dark navy one. In the pocket he found cigarettes, a lighter, sunglasses. Martyn, lingering for a parting shot, reminded him with slight triumph, 'I thought you were a bit *too* interested yesterday.'

He sent her a scathing look, put on his sun-glasses, took a cigarette from the packet, and as he lit it said carelessly, 'I gave you some avuncular advice, that's all. Now, on your way, mermaid.'

Martyn turned her back on him and marched off.

Next day Bastian didn't appear on the beach. She had watched from the window and she was conscious of a certain sadness that their friendship had ended so needlessly and so abruptly. When she was quite sure he wasn't coming, she walked along the beach by herself, and then she sprawled idly in the sun, the legs of her jeans rolled up, her cheek supported by a cushion of soft warm sand, the sun burning down on her with its steady loving heat. She was smarting from several hurts and yet she thought persistently of a man with black hair and grey eyes and a tanned face who had said, 'On your way, mermaid'. Who had said he had no taste for waterbabies. Who had thought yesterday that she was chasing him into the sea . . .

When at last she staggered up to go back home – because she was excruciatingly hungry – her legs and arms and one cheek were freckled with the glistening clinging fragments of shell and coral that made up the golden sand. She looked about her as she swung across the beach, but she didn't see that man. She wondered uneasily if he would be there at Julia Fleet's again, and she told herself she didn't care a jot either way. 'He's not my type,' she thought decidedly.

Back home, she made herself an enormous salad and added some cold meat left over from last night. She drank her usual glass of milk, and went outside to fetch in her black swimsuit. It was too early yet to leave for the Fleets', so she went to her room and brushed and brushed her hair. She had washed it this morning under the shower, so it was free of salt, soft and silky. She studied her reflection for a moment, then went into Rosalind's room to borrow some of her waterproof eye-shadow and mascara. Just for something to do, she told herself, and looked critically in the mirror to see what difference it made to her appearance. It added a touch of sophistication, she decided, and she could do with *that*.

Ready at last, and too impatient to sit around waiting, she decided to forget the bus and walk up to the plateau, despite the heat.

When she reached the Fleets' house, she went straight to the side garden where the pool was, because by now she was five minutes late and they would be ready and waiting for her.

But they weren't, and she stood stock still and stared.

Mrs. Fleet, Tom and Nanda – none of them were there. But *he* was, sitting in a cane chair wearing white shorts, his brown torso bare; smoking, and leafing through a magazine that looked like *The Land*. He looked up when she appeared, his dark eyebrows lifting.

Martyn swung her beach bag and said carelessly, 'You again! Where are Tom and Nanda?'

'Their mother's taken them to Manly to the dentist. Why do you ask?' he said maddeningly.

Martyn's heart jumped a little. Something was wrong! Perhaps one of the children had bad toothache. But – both of them? And they hadn't let her know not to come? She raised her darkened eyebrows slightly. 'Why do you think? I'm expecting to give them a lesson.'

He smiled faintly and folded his magazine firmly open. 'Then someone's slipped up. And I'm afraid it's you.'

'What?' Martyn stared at him blankly, trying to take it in. And then the truth struck her – she had come on the wrong day! However had she come to make such a silly mistake? And to have this man witness it. She said idiotically, 'What day is it?'

'Do you really not know? Or are you fooling? It's Thursday.'

'I thought it was Friday,' she said lamely, colouring deeply and furious with herself for the mistake. Particularly as it was plain now he didn't believe her. He made no comment but drew on his cigarette, and she noted abstractedly that he was as deeply and darkly suntanned as anyone she had seen up the coast. Legs and arms that were all muscle, a chest so broad and deep she wouldn't mind betting he could just about swim across the Pacific Ocean and back without drawing a new breath. 'You'd have got on with Stan,' she thought irrelevantly. But with Martyn Verity – nix! Yet if things had been otherwise –

She jumped when he remarked, 'You *are* done up today, aren't you! Like a dog's dinner. I hope you're not drooping those lovely painted lids for my benefit.'

'Sorry, not a chance of it,' she said tartly. She looked at the lovely beckoning blue of the pool and sighed frustratedly. No children, no lesson. Without bothering about good-byes, she began to move off when he said unexpectedly, 'The water looks good, doesn't it? Go ahead and have a swim before you leave. Don't let me put you off – what's your name again?'

'Martyn Verity,' she said warily, and taken by surprise.

'Well, then, Verity' – it was a deliberate mistake, she was sure – 'jump in and cool down and I'll see if I can find you a lemonade.'

She smouldered inwardly. Cool down! He was the most aggravating person she had ever met. And offering her lemonade! She said, 'My first name's Martyn – M-a-r-t-y-n. And you needn't put yourself out fetching lemonade. I can live without it.'

'Fine. Well, the pool's ready and waiting,' he reminded her mockingly.

She stood irresolute, unsure of what to do. To about-face would maybe seem childish, and the pool did look inviting. She wouldn't mind a swim.

His eyes flicked over her – the clean off-white jeans, the dark violet hand-crocheted top – a cast-off of Rosalind's, as a matter of fact – that showed her smooth brown shoulders. 'You're a ball of muscle, aren't you?' he commented, and returned to his reading.

With a shrug, and slightly disconcerted, Martyn moved away. She might as well have a swim. She had walked all this way for nothing otherwise. The back door of the house was open, and in the bathroom she changed into her black cotton swimsuit. She caught a glimpse of her face in the mirror and looked again. Done up like a dog's dinner! It was hardly flattering – and she didn't think she'd made a bad job of it. She hoped that eye make-up really was waterproof. If it wasn't, she was going to look a sight. But she wasn't going to wash it off and have him laugh to himself. He probably wasn't going to pay any more attention to her anyhow. He wasn't going to bother watching a kid like her swimming about in a pool.

'I should have just gone home,' she thought a little dismally, and wondered why she was letting herself in for this. She wondered too how it had happened she'd come here on the wrong day. That was something she'd never done before. She was uncomfortably sure that Dick, being a psychologist, would find some unpalatable and unacceptable answer to that one. Such as that she really wanted to see the nameless man out there. Which she definitely didn't ...

He didn't even look up from his reading when she re-appeared. 'Great,' thought Martyn. She dived into the water and swam up and down several times. Then she swam a couple of lengths underwater. She could hold her breath longer than most girls she knew, and she thought she might even have managed another half a length, but she didn't want to come up spluttering. This time when she emerged, he was watching her for the first time. If her make-up had run, then he was going to make some caustic comment. She pulled herself out on to the tiles and sat, her legs in the water, facing him.

'Not a bad swimmer, are you?' he said. He got to his feet and looked across the corner of the pool at her. 'What's the latest bulletin on the love affair? You didn't tell me yesterday.'

She blinked with shock at the unexpected question. 'There's no bulletin,' she said unco-operatively.

'None? Or do you just mean, Mind your own business? I've a good mind to read you another lecture. Maybe I would if you were dressed in something other than that cotton racing costume ... Well, I'll see about your lolly water.'

He disappeared and after a moment she got up, found her towel, and gave her hair a good rubbing. Then she carefully draped the towel around her shoulders and stood in the sunshine.

When he came back he brought a tray which he de-posited on a small white garden table on the lawn. Besides lemonade, he had brought a bottle of whisky and a small jug of ice. For himself, of course, not for her. So he was going to drink with her. But if he thought she was going to listen to another berating, then he was mistaken.

He looked over at her. He had got into a dark open-necked shirt while he was away though he still wore the white shorts. 'Come on,' he ordered. 'Sit down. I'll pour your drink.'

Martyn stayed where she was. 'If you plan on giving me a talking to,' she said decidedly, 'I'll drink my *lolly water* here – standing up. And then I'll go. I don't want to hear.'

His lip curled. 'Sit down,' he repeated. And as he didn't bring her glass across to her she moved the few paces reluctantly and sat. He fixed his drink, and she swallowed down her lemonade and poured herself another glass, and neither of them said anything. Then he remarked reflectively, 'Why don't you find some intelligent and profitable way of filling in time while you're learning about love? Believe me, you've got a long time to wait before you find the right man.'

'Really?' She fiddled with her glass and felt her cheeks burning. Here came the lecture! 'How would *you* know?'

'How do you suppose? You're not unique – and you're certainly not the first besotted young girl I've been acquainted with. Apart from anyone else, I have three younger sisters who've all gone through the vicissitudes of love.'

'I suppose you advised them all,' said Martyn sceptically. 'And they took your advice and are all now as happy as can be.'

He smiled slightly. 'I advised two of them,' he admitted. 'Not Julia who's the wildest and was married before the old man died. But the other two – yes, I gave them some advice on various occasions. One of them is now happily married, the other, Jan, is still having problems.'

'Surely you can solve them for her,' Martyn suggested pertly. 'I'd like to know what makes you such an expert, anyhow – seeing you're not even married. Are you a councillor or something?'

'I'm a cattleman,' he said, a glint of hard amusement in his grey eyes. 'I'm not an expert on love, but some things are pretty basic. I've had my share of love affairs – one at a time, by the way – and maturity is the greatest teacher

44

of all. As for you, my guess is you're still struggling through the very first primer.'

As he finished speaking he got leisurely to his feet, and glancing round, Martyn discovered that someone else had come into the garden. Not Julia Fleet, but a small trim middle-aged woman with dark hair, who was coming towards them with a quick and lively step. Martyn was aware of curiously confused feelings – of slight annoyance at the interruption, because despite herself her imagination was piqued by his statement that he was a cattleman; of relief that she wasn't going to have to battle on with this conversation. She would have fallen off her chair if she had known that this same woman was going to start wheels turning that would change the whole of her future life.

# CHAPTER THREE

'You're back early, Poppy,' observed the dark man. 'How's Jan? Thinking over my suggestions?'

The woman called Poppy gave a little rueful smile. She had a lively, very likeable face, her eyes behind prettily framed glasses were dark brown and intelligent, and before she answered she looked with friendly curiosity at Martyn, who had stood up too.

'Jan wants to come to Diamond Springs with me, now. I'll tell you all about it later ... Are you going to introduce me to your friend, Tancred?'

Tancred! Martyn had vague schoolgirl memories of a Tancred who had imprisoned Richard the Lionheart during one of the Crusades, and she wondered briefly if it was a suitable name. She felt a spark of malicious amusement at being referred to as Tancred's friend, but she supposed he would soon straighten out *that* little error.

Only of course he was not sufficiently interested.

He merely said offhandedly, rather surprisingly getting her name right, 'This is Martyn Verity. She's been teaching Tom and Nanda to swim, but she came on the wrong day ... Martyn, my stepmother, Mrs. Diamond.'

Diamond Springs, Tancred Diamond – diamond-hard eyes, thought Martyn abstractedly as he and the older woman smiled at each other. There was something alert and thoughtful in Poppy Diamond's glance at Martyn, standing there in her black swimsuit, the striped towel draped across her shoulders and covering her breast. Then she sank down in one of the cane chairs exclaiming, 'Lovely cool drinks! Tancred, I'd love a long, long lime and soda with just the slightest, tiniest dash of gin. I'm feeling absolutely whacked after wrestling with poor Jan and her problems all afternoon.'

He said nothing, but disappeared, presumably to fetch

the drink. Martyn was thinking, 'Jan – that's the sister he mentioned before.' She stood irresolute, feeling uncomfortably that she was intruding on a family scene, and that this woman must want to talk to her stepson about his sister. She said politely, 'I think I'd better be going, Mrs. Diamond.'

'Going? When we've just met? Oh, don't do that. Sit down and tell me about yourself. Did you meet Red here at Julia's?'

Red? Tancred – Red Diamond! He was black rather than Red, thought Martyn – She said, 'Yes. And then we met down on the beach, but—' She stopped. That was enough to say. She hoped she wasn't going to be asked if she liked him, or even to agree that he was – well, to agree that he was anything that was in his favour. Because personally she found him infuriating and just too superior for words.

'Now sit down, Martyn. That's an unusual name, by the way. It somehow suits you. Pour yourself another drink. Is it really lemonade?' She sounded amused, and Martyn, remembering her eye make-up, wondered if she was taken for being rather more than nineteen years old. Old enough anyhow for this woman to think she was a friend of Tancred's. More than a mere waterbaby. Adult – and past being satisfied with lemonade.

She said, 'Yes, it's lemonade. I've been walking and swimming, and I was thirsty.' With sudden honesty she added, regardless of sense or sequence, 'He – Red – and I only met on the beach by accident.'

Poppy raised her eyebrows slightly and looked amused. 'I don't believe in accidents – of that kind. There's usually a bit of planning behind them.'

Mine, thought Martyn, chagrined. She was the one who had chased him into the water. But his stepmother presumably took it for granted that any planning had been done by *him*.

'Anyhow,' said Poppy, further amused by her obvious embarrassment, 'here's Tancred with my drink.'

The drink delivered, Red Diamond said, 'Excuse me, I'm going in to dress. I'll leave you two to talk. You can tell me about Jan later, Poppy.' And he disappeared.

Poppy sipped her drink gratefully. 'I'm sorry about this – turning up at the wrong time. You'd reached the stage of talking about an eternally fascinating subject – love.'

Martyn coloured. 'Not really. He was – your stepson was – just advising me—'

Poppy held up one hand and smiled. 'Sh! I don't want to pry ... Tell me about this swimming business instead. I never did learn to swim. Is your teaching a full-time occupation or is a sort of holiday job?'

'Neither really,' Martyn admitted. 'It's just sort of part-time. It doesn't even earn enough to keep me,' she added honestly. And then, without quite knowing how it had happened, she was telling Poppy Diamond about Stan and how she had come to live with Ros and Dick, and how she had to find a better way of earning a living very soon.

'The only thing anyone can think of is typing,' she confessed, leaning back now and sipping lemonade no longer ice-cold, stretching out her bare brown legs and feeling more at ease. 'But—'

'But you're an outdoor girl. Not a city girl?'

'I was brought up on the north coast.' A little more encouragement and she was talking about Stan again, and how different life with him had been.

'Ros thinks I've been spoiled – and that I'm a barbarian. And I suppose she's right.'

'You're in a period of adjustment,' said the older woman when she paused. 'Never mind. It will all sort itself out.'

'Yes – except I can't wait for that,' Martyn agreed. 'Ros has given me a week – that's just a few days now – to work something out. I suppose it's fair enough. I have to do something – everyone does. And I expect lots of them do things they don't really want to do. It'll be secretarial school for me,' she concluded with a grimace.

'That would be a pity, when you're an athletic type.'
There was a short pause, then Poppy Diamond looked directly at Martyn. 'Would you be at all interested in coming to Diamond Springs?'

'What?' Martyn's blue eyes widened in surprise. She felt flabbergasted. 'Diamond Springs?' she repeated uncomprehendingly. A cattleman, she thought—

'Red must have told you that the Diamonds are outback people – cattle station owners.'

'Sort of,' said Martyn faintly. It began to strike her as faintly funny that she was being invited to Diamond Springs, in the circumstances. It was a good thing Red was not present to hear it!

Poppy Diamond had narrowed her brown eyes as if she were thinking, and while those eyes were not actually focused on Martyn, it was as if they were intent on her in some peculiar way and the girl moved uncomfortably.

'Yes, I think I have a plan that could possibly suit us both. Admirably. Though of course it's no use if the very thought of the outback horrifies you. Does it?'

'Of course not,' said Martyn rashly. She had never been far away from the sea, but outback was a magical word, and no matter what her other thoughts, it was one that sent prickles of excitement running up and down her spine. It was just a pity it had to be associated in any way with Red Diamond. 'It doesn't horrify me at all.'

'Well then.' Poppy paused for thought again. 'I'm planning to spend three or four weeks at Diamond Springs. Would that be a breathing space for you – long enough for you to work something out to suit yourself? I'd try to help too,' she promised.

Martyn frowned. 'It's very kind of you, but – but I don't see why you should bother about me. Besides—' She stopped. Why bring her hostile relationship with Red into it?

'I'm not being entirely altruistic,' Poppy assured her. 'I'm being logical too. Believe me, I think things out, and

I think them quickly. It's one of my few strong points. I'll explain . . . You heard Red asking about his sister—'

'Jan?'

'Yes. He may have told you she's been in a motor accident, and that she's broken off her engagement. Now she wants to come home to Diamond Springs – to get away from it all, and to recuperate. She's round about your age – twenty-one – and she needs young company. Her leg is not all that bad, and the doctor confirms that one of the best ways of rebuilding the muscle is swimming. Well, she can swim at Diamond Springs – there's a good pool there – but how much swimming is she likely to do on her own? Red's busy, and I'm just not a swimmer – I'd drown if I fell into two inches of water. The only time I cross a river is when there's a drought. So do you see? She's set on coming outback, and if you would come too, it might stop us all from going bananas – you with your problem, me with mine, making it all possible for Jan. Isn't that logic?'

It was, of course. But it was still impossible. Martyn said, 'But you don't know a thing about me.'

'Now come *on*! When you've been telling me all about yourself for the past ten minutes – when Julia trusts you with her children! When you and I are so obviously *simpatico*! No, Martyn, I'm a woman who makes quick decisions about people and I'm seldom wrong.'

'But—' began Martyn helplessly.

'No buts. You'll never persuade me you're a doubtful character. Not with those ultra-honest eyes. And I'll tell you something else, Martyn. I married Red's father eleven years ago, and do you know how long I'd known him? I'd met him exactly twice. Once was at a picnic race meeting, the second time was the day after at a dinner party. And neither of us had a single regret in the five years of married life we shared. And all I'm trying to point out in telling you that is that I'm quite capable of making a quick and accurate judgment of character . . . Anyhow, think it all over, will you? When will you be here again?'

'Tomorrow. It's the last lesson.'

'Tomorrow, then,' said Poppy with finality. 'I'm not giving you a week – just a day's long enough. And I hope you'll say yes.' When Red came back a minute later she remarked, 'You've taken your time, Tancred. Never mind – Martyn and I have really got to know each other, haven't we, Martyn? You'd be surprised.'

Martyn felt too stunned to answer. Poppy's invitation had really put her in a spot. Of course she wanted to go to the outback, and yet her conscious mind warned her darkly, 'With that man there? Never! It would *never* do.' She felt those *diamond*-bright eyes on her, and she wondered if they were hostile or merely sceptical. She raised her eyes to meet his gaze fully and could almost hear his question – 'What have you been up to while I've been away?' But all he said was a laconic, 'If you run along and make yourself decent, I'll drive you home, Martyn.'

It was the first time he had actually called her Martyn, and it gave her a peculiar sensation. Though she couldn't think why it should be so.

She wondered as she changed out of her swimsuit if Poppy – Poppy? Mrs Diamond! – was at this very minute telling him all about her brilliant idea. Well, he would quash it, for sure. But she would get in first – he wasn't going to dictate to her, to win another victory. She would tell Poppy she had decided she couldn't come, and she would tell her today – before she left. She didn't care a cent if Red Diamond realized her refusal was on account of him. On the contrary, in fact. She thought briefly of Jan – the motor accident, the broken engagement, the swimming that would help her injured leg. But she couldn't possibly do it, worse luck. Because the outback – well, it would have been fascinating to go there.

Dressed, she flicked a comb through her now dry hair and fastened it back. The make-up was as good as new, and she looked easily twenty-one. Poppy had thought that. She liked Poppy, and that was a shame too. It would have been nice to be able to help.

When she went back outside, he was waiting for her, but Poppy had simply disappeared, so Martyn had no chance of voicing the refusal she had planned. In no time at all she was alone in the car with Red, being driven home.

He didn't waste any time at all in letting her know that Poppy had let him in on her bright idea – or in giving her his opinion on the subject.

'You told me an hour ago there's no bulletin on your current amour. Now I don't know what the hell that meant, but this new idea of dropping everything and falling in with my stepmother's impulsive plans – storming the outback – that's utterly out of the question. Just what's in your mind? I assure you there's no amusement in store for you at Diamond Springs. You'd better tell my stepmother tomorrow that you're not coming.'

He hadn't looked at her at all, he simply talked fast and drove fast, down towards the sea.

Martyn had already made up her mind that she couldn't go to Diamond Springs – simply because it would mean putting up with *him*. But she certainly wasn't going to let him tell her what to do. She wasn't dense, and she had the distinct impression that he imagined she had ideas of amusing herself with him. He had already accused her of chasing him into the sea and warned her not to attach herself to him. Well, he appeared to have an opinion of his own attractions that was just too conceited for words. He wasn't even what you would call good-looking! He was too dark and tough – certainly not the type of man she would ever dream about. If he didn't like waterbabies, nor did she like big-headed cattlemen. It was a pity, though, that she had ever been silly enough to blurt out so gratuitously that Bastian Sinclair wanted to marry her. That had really got her offsides with him!

She drew a deep breath and told him with all the composure she could muster, 'Here's what's in my mind, Mr. Diamond. Or rather, who is. And that's your sister Jan.

52

She's the one and only reason I could just possibly consider coming to Diamond Springs. You see, swimming just happens to be great exercise for people in all sorts of conditions, if properly supervised. It's not too strenuous, because water supports the body. It's the one thing I know backwards, and if swimming's needed to help your sister recover from her accident, then this could be just the – intelligent time-filler you said I needed, couldn't it?' She sent him a triumphant glance and concluded, 'I know you think I'm a silly kid with nothing in my head but love affairs, but even a big-time cattleman can't always be right.'

There was a second's silence. 'So it would seem,' he said. 'However, you could have spared me the pseudo-scientific speechifying.' Then – 'You look like emerging as something of an enigma. I find it difficult to make sense of you.'

'I'm not asking you to make sense of me,' retorted Martyn, feeling she had really scored a point this time. 'We just aren't – *simpatico*, are we?' she added bitingly.

'You express my thoughts exactly,' he agreed lightly. 'Unfortunately, I can't see you keeping altogether out of my way at Diamond Springs – you won't be spending all your time at the billabong. So do me a favour, will you, and tell my stepmother no.'

By now they had reached the point where he would let Martyn out of the car, and her hand was ready on the door. As she got out, she said offhandedly, 'No is your favourite word for me, isn't it? Sorry – I'm not particularly interested in doing you a favour – you're not the one I'm aiming to please ... Thanks for the lift. Goodbye.' And without a backward glance, she walked quickly towards the bungalow.

What a positively detestable man, she thought. The calm, arrogant way he had told her to say No – for the second time – made her almost determined to say yes, just to aggravate him. After all, Poppy had asked her along mainly for Jan's sake. The fact that it would also, temporarily at least, be helpful to Martyn was only of secondary importance. Yet to go would, in a way, be cutting off her nose to spite her face. She didn't think she could put up for long with that man even in very small doses.

Well, she would think it through carefully and reasonably, weighing all the pros and cons, after dinner. She would take a calming walk by the sea, and there she would get the whole thing into perspective and decide what it was worth to her. She had always loved walking by the sea at night, hearing the softened roar of the waves as they creamed stealthily in over the sands – gently, peacefully, after their restless flaunting power of the day. She loved to feel the softness of the night air flowing over her limbs and face, and to see the stars hanging in the darkness of the heavens, remote and mysterious and beautiful as they had been before man had learned too much and landed on the moon.

But as it happened, she didn't do any quiet thinking after dinner. Unexpectedly, her mind was made up for her when her brother came into the kitchen to dry the dishes for her.

She had a feeling Rosalind had sent him along – to finalize things. She had been very conscious during dinner that she was an intruder in the house, a positive pain in the neck to Ros, who could probably visualize her staying for ever and ever. She sympathized with Ros quite heartily and wished herself free and independent, and years and years older. Unfortunately, she had never been the sort of girl who is ready at eighteen to kiss her parents goodbye and go out into the world. All in all, she thought it had been pretty noble of Ros to put up with her so long. But the irritations were beginning to surface now, and tonight she had been home too late, and the *pot-au-feu* had not been properly cooked. How to explain that she had mistaken the day and gone to give a swimming lesson that was scheduled for tomorrow?

'Well, Bit,' Richard said with a kind of cheerful determination, 'have you made any weighty decisions about this career of yours? It just won't do for you to continue with this aimless, lazy life, you know.'

Martyn listened to him a little regretfully. She thought that, if she could get to know him well, she would quite like this brother of hers. But it wasn't going to advance their relationship if she stayed here too long.

She admitted, 'I haven't really, Dick. I'm sorry. I know that the swimming's not enough, but apart from that and drawing and helping at the baths, I don't seem to have any particular talents.'

He frowned slightly. He had a rather austere and scholarly face – not in the least like Stan's – but there was a little softness, and a lot of concern – for Ros? for her? – in his blue eyes. He said briskly, 'Neither swimming nor drawing's going to make a living for you. I think we'll just have to make your mind up for you. And I'm pretty sure you'll find that after all there's nothing so deadly dull about secretarial work. There are a lots of jobs to choose from, and I'll possibly be able to wangle something interesting for you one way or another. So what do you say? Shall we arrange for you to start next week, if possible?'

'No.' Martyn said it so determinedly that she gave even herself a start. 'I don't want to do typing. How would you have liked it if Stan had said you had to be a – a plumber, or a dentist or something, when you wanted to be a psychologist?' He was staring at her as if she had suddenly changed into a hobgoblin or something, and she hurried on, 'But don't worry, I won't bug you any longer than I can possibly help. I'll think of something, and in the meantime, I've – I've been invited to stay at a cattle station, anyhow.'

'Who on earth by?' he exploded. 'What's this all about? Now look here, Bit, what have you been up to all day on your own?'

Martyn bit her lip. 'It's too late to go into all that now,

isn't it?' she said, thinking of Bastian and the bother she *could* have struck there, in her innocence. Then at the alarm in his face, she reassured him, 'But it's perfectly all right, Dick. Don't get apoplectic. I've been invited outback by the grandmother of some kids I've been teaching, that's all.'

'*Is* it all?' Richard looked quite fierce. 'Well, before you start making any arrangements, I'd like to meet this grandmother and find out what it's all about. You're not in search of a holiday, you know, Bit. We're trying to bring you down to earth.'

'But too quickly,' Martyn protested. Now she had said she was going outback, she knew she wouldn't go back on it. Her mind was made up, and Red Diamond could go jump in the lake or the billabong or the dam, or something, if he didn't like the idea of her 'storming' his cattle station. 'I know I'm a problem to you, Dickie. I suppose I'm just – slow at growing up, but I can't help it. I can't sort it all out in a few days, and I *do* want to get out of Ros's hair—' Suddenly there were tears in her eyes despite her defiance, and Richard, who naturally had more feeling for her than his wife, softened at once.

He said clumsily, 'Don't cry about it, Bit. It's a pity you don't fit in with us, but you just don't and that's all. So as long as I meet this woman and can be sure there's no funny business—'

Martyn dried her eyes and smiled a little. 'There's absolutely no funny business, Dick.' She didn't really think Red Diamond would qualify as 'funny business'! – and anyhow, he simply didn't come into her plans, and when she talked further to Dick about the reason why she had been invited to Diamond Springs, she didn't even give him a mention . . .

To her relief, he wasn't there the following day when she went to Julia Fleet's. Poppy was delighted she had decided to accept her invitation and agreed to come and meet Rosalind and Richard the next day, and plans were outlined. Tuesday Poppy would pick her up at the bungalow to go to Kingsford Smith airport. Poppy would arrange the flight and the expense would be hers.

'Bring enough clothes for a month, and remember it will be hot and you'll be doing lots of swimming – and some riding too, if you'd care to.' Martyn didn't mention Red and his injunctions not to come. He might be the boss of the cattle station, but this was between her and Poppy. Diamond Springs, Poppy told her, was way out west. 'Too far from the coast, really. After my husband died, I left Red in charge – well, he'd taken over a year previously, really – and came to Sydney with the girls. Julia was married, but Belinda was at university and Jan was still at school, and I reckoned they needed me more than he did. You can imagine – Red wouldn't want an organizing stepmother around the place. He's a very competent man,' she added, and Martyn forbore to comment.

Ros and Richard were both impressed by Poppy Diamond, though Ros made the point that this was to be a breathing space only for Martyn, who when she came back would have to knuckle down to secretarial school if she hadn't found any suitable alternative. Poppy listened seriously, and said she was sure everything would work out satisfactorily.

'She's a nice woman. Sensible too,' Rosalind remarked when Poppy had gone. 'You're lucky, Bit – and lucky we're letting you go off on a holiday like this. Because for sure it's going to be more holiday than work. I wonder who runs Diamond Springs?' She paused, and Martyn shrugged as if she hadn't a clue. 'I just hope you might meet some nice uncomplicated outdoor type there, and get married. That would solve everyone's worries, wouldn't it?'

Martyn supposed it would, but she couldn't see it happening. Besides, after her brief experience with Bastian, she didn't really think she was ready for love and marriage. Red Diamond was right – she had years to wait for the right man, and she liked it that way. She didn't care

57

how slowly she was developing. Her main problem was going to be how to fill in the years between, and she thought for the first time in days of that children's book she used to talk about. *Not* an acceptable alternative to knuckling down to hard work, of course.

Ros and Richard had rather alarmingly decided Martyn should have some new clothes, as she had nothing sophisticated at all apart from a few of Ros's cast-offs, and though she protested, Rosalind took Monday off from work and accompanied her to town. There, her sister-in-law selected clothes for Martyn that she considered suitable for the country, and Martyn wondered secretly if she would ever feel at home in them. She was quite sure she would never wear either of the two pretty semi-evening dresses. She had the uneasy feeling that Ros had that 'uncomplicated outdoor type' very much in mind, particularly when she insisted Martyn should have her hair professionally styled at a hairdressing salon – for the first time in her life.

She hardly recognized herself with her shorter, sleeker, cleverly cut hairstyle. Was this *blonde* the waterbaby from the north coast? It had been no use protesting that it was all costing too much. 'Your father left you a little money, Bit – you're not completely penniless,' she was reminded.

'Maybe I should have told Poppy no,' she thought once or twice. But it was too late now, and besides, it would have been straight off to secretarial school, and as well, she'd have stayed under Ros's feet. Everyone was much more pleased with her this way.

Everyone, that is, but Red Diamond. She didn't expect *he* would be exactly delighted when she turned up with Poppy and Jan.

Tuesday morning after Ros and Richard had wished her a happy time and gone to work – and reminded her to lock up carefully – she spotted Bastian and Becky on the beach, and on an impulse went over the fence to say goodbye. Bastian stared when he saw her in the pretty faded-rose knitted cotton dress that Ros had instructed her she was to wear on the flight.

'Martyn! You're bewilderingly beautiful. And your hair – you've had four inches cut off it. But what style! What's happened in your life that you're suddenly so grown up? I'm prepared to believe you've taken up fashion modelling.'

Martyn felt embarrassed at what she saw in his eyes. Covetousness. Desire. And she would die of horror if he kissed her good-bye. She said quickly, keeping her distance while even Becky stared in puzzlement instead of jumping up, 'I'm going away. I thought I'd say good-bye. I've got a sort of job in the country – a temporary one. Teaching a girl to swim,' she added, simplifying it so he would not start asking questions.

He was still looking at her. 'I've missed you. When you come back, look me up, won't you? Both of us might be interested in love, marriage, by then. I'm an emotional cripple at the moment, having just finished with one marriage.'

And another love affair? she wondered, even while she told him, 'I don't want to get married for years and years.'

'If you should change your mind, think of me then. Give me first option,' he said lightly, and added, 'You're lovely! Really lovely. Do I get a good-bye kiss?'

She said awkwardly, 'I'd rather not,' and wondered what had made her force this encounter. To try herself out in her new guise? She didn't like the thought. 'I have to go – I haven't finished my packing and I mustn't leave my bedroom in a mess.'

It was a relief to get away, and yet she thought about him when she was safely back at the bungalow. He had looked at her differently – *so* differently. As if she were a woman with – she sought for words to express. A woman with a woman's power. Whereas before she had been completely at his mercy. But she wasn't a woman. She didn't have a woman's power. It was all on the outside.

59

Clothes, a new hairstyle, make-up. Inside she was as unsophisticated as ever. She still didn't know the first thing about love, and she knew *his* kisses couldn't teach her that . . .

When the taxi came at last, Poppy Diamond was the sole passenger. Without being entirely aware of it, she had been tensed up to face Red and Jan, and it was a relief as well as an anticlimax when they were not there. Poppy confessed to hating flying, and was all nerves, and though in the taxi Martyn babbled with determined cheerfulness about her new clothes and her excitement and so on, she knew that the other woman took in scarcely a syllable of it. At Kingsford Smith airport, once they had checked in their luggage – Poppy had two suitcases, both of them surprisingly large, Martyn one, brand new, very smart, and bought yesterday – they went for coffee.

Poppy swallowed down a tablet with hers. 'It will make me dopey, but it can't be helped. I can't face the trip without it. I hope you're a good air traveller, Martyn.'

For Martyn Verity, this was the first air trip she had ever made, but now didn't seem quite the time to admit it, so she merely smiled and said, 'You don't have to worry about me – I'll be perfectly okay.'

It was not till some time after they were airborne and Poppy was dozing – or appeared to be – that Martyn got round to thinking about Jan and Red again. They must have left a day or so earlier, but she was determined not to spoil her enjoyment of the flight by thinking about the meeting ahead of her. With Red, of course. She was looking forward to meeting Jan and making friends with her. She couldn't possibly be anything like her brother!

Looking down from the air she marvelled at her first ever sight of anywhere from this high up. It was fantastic. First there had been the sea, sparkling, blue, patterned like fish scales, as the plane flew east; then they wheeled around to fly west over the city, then over a floor of white cloud and across the ranges and the tablelands. Finally the plains, incredible flatness and emptiness, fewer and fewer signs of habitation. Martyn looked down, reading rivers from lines, scrub from dots, homesteads from tiny cubes, towns from glittering iron roofs. The sea was hundreds of miles away, and she wondered if she was going to miss it terribly.

At last they put down at an outback airfield, and from there they had to take a feeder flight. Poppy was groggy and uncommunicative and able only to stagger from one aircraft to the other, and Martyn felt sorry for her. For her part, she was feeling on the tips of her toes – elated, excited, amazed at her own good fortune. The *outback*! And here it was, first of all, around them in the hot dry air that was so different from the moist coastal air; in the small isolated airfield, and then below them again after they had boarded the little feeder plane. It was a fairly smooth ride, but Poppy looked sick and kept her eyes closed, and Martyn wasn't able to ask her any questions about the country they were passing over where away below, on red earth patched with green and grey, she could see the thin silver line of a river, the shimmer of a dam, the red or silver-roofed buildings in their surrounds of toy trees that were homesteads.

Something in her heart began to sing. She had forsaken the sea, her first love, for this adventure, and it was going to be wonderful, in spite of everything. Everything meaning Red Diamond.

They came down in the middle of nowhere – or so one would have thought. Though Martyn had seen a tiny town – a straggle of houses with galvanized iron roofs that glittered in the sun – and the red ribbon of a road.

Poppy opened her eyes as the plane bumped to a standstill. 'Thank God that's over!' And then it was no time till they were out in the sizzling heat and a big dark man was striding across to meet them. Red. Martyn's heart beat out a small tattoo of apprehension.

He kissed his stepmother briefly on the cheek and looked at Martyn twice as if checking who she was. The first time with interest, foxed, she thought, by the dress and four inches off her straw-coloured hair; the second time with animosity and cold condemnation. He gave her an unsmiling nod and then proceeded to ignore her.

'Are you all right, Poppy? You don't look *quite* as green as usual ... My God, whose is all this luggage?' His raised brows and silver sharp glance told Martyn he thought it was hers, and she said quickly, defensively, 'I've just the one case – I'll take it.'

'Oh, the brand new one,' he said sardonically. 'The honeymoon one.' His eyes, screwed up in the fiercely bright sunlight, flicked over her as ungently as naked blades, and he remarked so that only she could hear it, for Poppy was moving groggily ahead, 'And you're done up to match it, aren't you, Martyn Verity?'

She crimsoned and hated him. He looked broader, bigger, darker than she remembered, and his thick black hair gave him a barbaric air. No, she thought, he certainly didn't have film-star looks. He was horribly tough and hard. Jan, she presumed, had been left behind at the homestead. Ignoring his gibe, she asked, 'Do we have far to drive?'

'Forty odd miles.' He added, 'You certainly made up your mind to get here, didn't you?'

'I certainly did,' she agreed, her head up. 'Everyone doesn't have to take your advice, you see.'

Poppy was waiting and now they had reached his car – a station wagon. Red allocated the seats, Poppy in the front – 'I want to talk to you about Jan' – Martyn in the back. Well, that suited Martyn, who was now feeling really jumpy and on edge. It was the unpleasant effect Red Diamond had on her. She hoped he wasn't going to make life miserable for her just because she hadn't been intimidated by him. She was going to listen to what they said in the front seat, anyhow, and she didn't care if he knew it. Anything about Jan must be of interest to her, since the object of her coming here was to be helpful.

They didn't talk at all at first. Poppy was leaning back against the seat and had asked for ten minutes' peace to settle her nerves. Martyn stared out at the scenery. Red earth, gum trees, plains that stretched to infinity. A sun that had a different brilliance from the sun at the coast, because here it was reflected back from a different coloured landscape. The road was rough, and it was a long time before she saw any cattle at all. Once there was a river – wide, with sloping red banks shaded by great gum trees. The road went straight across, and the brown water splashed coolly and noisily up around the station wagon. A few dragonflies darted about, and some white cock-atoos flew against the blue of the sky, and finally Poppy sat up straight and ran her fingers through her hair and sighed. The man beside her remarked almost at once, 'Feeling better?' Then, 'I took it for granted you'd have come unaccompanied.'

Martyn didn't hear the first part of Poppy's reply, only, 'I'm always better not travelling alone, Red. You know that.'

Martyn saw him shrug his broad shoulders. Her cheeks were burning.

'Well, how about Jan?' he said after a moment.

Martyn moved fractionally forward in her seat. If she was going to be any use to Jan, then the more she knew about her the better, so she was going to listen hard.

She very soon discovered that she wasn't going to be any use at all, and that she didn't need to know even one tiny little thing about Jan Diamond.

Because Jan wasn't at Diamond Springs, and she wasn't coming.

# CHAPTER FOUR

MARTYN's blood ran cold. No Jan, no reason for Martyn Verity to have come to Diamond Springs.

Red had known, Poppy had known, but Martyn had not been told. She simply couldn't understand it. Why hadn't Poppy telephoned, or come to the bungalow and explained that she wasn't needed after all? Instead, she had simply arrived in the taxi, watched her and her luggage being loaded in, talked about the disagreeableness of air travel, and uttered not a single word about altered plans.

And Martyn had made an utter fool of herself with her pert retort to Red's unfriendly greeting.

Now here she was, an unwelcome, useless visitor to his domain. And she knew exactly what he must be thinking. She was chasing him – first into the ocean, now to the outback. It would be no use protesting, 'I came for Jan's sake'.

What had happened, she gathered from her eavesdropping – if it could be called that – was that Jan's engagement was on again. She had seen the doctor – 'after that stern lecture you gave her before you left, Tancred' – and this time she hadn't been over-emotional or refused to listen. She was convinced now she was going to be neither deformed nor a cripple, and when Barry turned up she at last agreed to see him. Result – she was wearing her ring again, and had gone off to Terrigal to stay with him and his parents, where she would have plenty of sun and sea and swimming and love, and be whole, body and mind, in no time.

Red listened to Poppy's recital in almost complete silence. 'So – happy ending,' Poppy concluded, and he nodded.

'When she rang that it was all on again I was relieved,

but I'm glad to have the details. Barry's a good bloke — definitely the man for Jan. I told her that, and confidentially, I told Barry too.'

Martyn in the back seat kept perfectly silent. She was glad that everything was ending happily for Jan, even though she didn't know the girl personally. But what she felt most keenly about was her own false position. The thought of that made her grit her teeth.

Poppy turned round and rested one arm along the back of the seat. She looked a better colour now, and she smiled brightly as she said, 'Sorry for excluding you, Martyn. I was just bringing Red up to date about Jan. Are you all right there?'

'Yes, thank you,' said Martyn stiffly. She thought, 'You could have brought *me* up to date too — before it was too late.' Why hadn't Poppy done that? And how on earth was she going to put in three or four weeks on Diamond Springs? Her heart sank at the prospect.

Somewhere along the line they went through gates and along a double red track that crossed an enormous paddock. Away off under some trees, Martyn saw cattle, and then there was another gate — horses — and beyond, on a slight rise, the homestead sheltering amongst trees, with a straggle of buildings a little way off where, she presumed, the stockmen and station-hands must be quartered.

She didn't know what sort of a homestead she had pictured, but this one was long and low, green-roofed, and surrounded by a very wide, open verandah with insect screens all round.

Someone came down from the verandah as they all moved from the car to the house — a grey-haired woman with a weather-worn face, who embraced Poppy and was introduced to Martyn as Mrs. Hall, the housekeeper. The two women went ahead talking into the house, and Martyn was left to follow with Red, who was carrying one of his stepmother's suitcases, and hers. She walked a little away from him, uneasy and resentful. She felt a fool, but she wasn't going to start protesting innocence. He could think what he liked. He'd soon discover she wanted as little as possible to do with him.

He said coldly, 'As Jan wasn't coming, we weren't expecting you, so we don't have a room ready, but Mrs. Hall will soon get one of the girls to make up the bed. Fortunately, we do have several empty bedrooms.'

Martyn swallowed, and said equally coldly, 'May I please have one a long way from yours?' and was only a little ashamed of her own rudeness.

'Certainly,' he said crisply. She followed him round the verandah. 'We'll put your things in here. It's the best I can do for distance. Tidy yourself up – hang up your clothes when you get them out of that beautiful honeymoon suitcase. There's a bathroom along the hall if you want to freshen up. We'll expect you on the verandah for a drink when you're ready. Are you sticking to lemonade or have you promoted yourself to stiff drinks?' His grey eyes quizzed her ironically.

She looked back at him for an instant, and she didn't see anything in his face that resembled in the slightest degree Bastian's expression when he had seen her in the faded-rose – and very expensive – outfit she now wore. For Red Diamond she certainly wasn't a woman with a woman's power. She was just an obnoxious – kid – whom he positively disliked.

She said with an attempt at bravado, 'To celebrate this particular occasion – yes, I think I'll promote myself to stiff drinks.'

He smiled slightly, cynically, and left her alone.

She didn't change. One thing she did, though, and that was take off her sheer tights. It was just too killingly hot in them. Then she went along to the bathroom for a wash. There was a clean face towel there and she removed the make-up she had put on earlier in the day – for what reason she could not now imagine. It was a fresh-looking, modern bathroom, everything was spotless. She thought it must be a second bathroom – a guests' bathroom. Somehow she hadn't thought there would be

66

such things on a cattle station. There certainly hadn't been in the tiny timber residence at the swimming baths, where she had lived with Stan! She felt a little afraid about what she had inadvertently let herself in for, and wondered if she would possibly be able to leave in a few days. If she did, what an ovation she would get from Ros and Richard, she *didn't* think! Especially when they had laid out all that money on her wardrobe – in hopes of the uncomplicated outdoor type she might meet!

Well, it was her money in a way, but seeing she had lived with them for over two months, she didn't really think they owed her anything. Dick had said earlier, 'We'll keep your money as a nest egg for you, Bit. Then when you need it, for training, or for anything special or extraordinary that arises, it will be there.' She thought her nest egg must have been diminished somewhat by this spending spree Ros had taken her on – for a special occasion!

When she came back from the bathroom it was almost dark and she had to grope for the light switch in the bedroom. She looked around the room for the first time. Muted blue bedspread and curtains, off-white walls, vinyl flooring in a pale pretty floral pattern, two simple string-coloured rugs. Funny after the rough and tumble with Stan up the coast, and the small room it had been a battle to keep tidy in Richard's house.

She went out to the verandah and walked around, and when she found a lighted area was relieved to find Poppy there alone. That man, who figured in her mind like some dark devil, wasn't in evidence. She said immediately, 'Mrs. Diamond, why didn't you tell me Jan wasn't coming? If I'd known, of course I wouldn't have come.'

Poppy was leaning back in a long chair of fine cane, looking very civilized and very composed – which she had not looked during the journey. She said wryly, 'Yes, that's why I didn't tell you. It *was* a little bit underhand of me, but I know you're going to love the outback, and you struck me at once as being just the girl for—' She passed

67

fractionally and then went on, 'For this sort of life. You'll soon discover the spell the country puts on you.' She smiled persuasively at Martyn, who stood with her back against the verandah rails, feeling on edge because she knew that Red would soon appear.

'Besides,' said Poppy, 'the idea was to be helpful to you too, wasn't it? You still have your little problem to solve.'

'Yes, but it's not *your* problem. You don't really *know* me, Mrs. Diamond, and Red—'

'Please call me Poppy,' the other woman interrupted. 'And don't worry about Red. We'll all soon get to know each other – though I feel I know you already ... Anyhow, I like to have another woman around the homestead when I'm here. It's good for Red, too. That's one reason I visit every so often, and I generally bring someone along.'

Martyn wasn't convinced. Mrs. Hall was here, and Poppy appeared to be on very good terms with her. She couldn't pretend to herself that having *her* here was going to be good for Red, and she wondered fleetingly who else Poppy had brought.

When Red appeared with sherry, she accepted a glass, ignored him, and looked out into the darkness. Dinner was ready so they didn't linger, and the meal was bearable because Poppy talked. About what, Martyn hardly knew. She was worried and she was tired and confused, though the sherry had picked her up a little. Poppy talked about somewhere called Jindi-yindi – 'That place has a hex on it,' she said. She talked about the extraordinary rains that had fallen in the past few weeks.

'Luckily we didn't get too much,' Red said. 'Parts of Jindi-yindi were just about swamped out.'

'I told you there's a hex on it. It's a place I'd leave *strictly* alone if I were you, Red.'

To Martyn, it sounded singularly like a challenge, but Red didn't answer it. His eyes sought her out across the table fleetingly, and then he told Poppy, 'It's quite like old times, isn't it?'

There was a tiny silence.

'What do you mean?' Poppy said.

He raised his dark eyebrows. 'When Jan and Linda came home for holidays, wasn't there always an extra girl or two as well?'

'Well, what's so wrong with that? There's not much company here. It's good for you.'

His eyes glittered and Martyn looked away. She thought, chilled and appalled, 'Girls invited here for *his* benefit—'

'What became of that last desperately eager girl, by the way?'

He reached across for the coffee jug, very casually, as he spoke. 'What was her name? Very pretty – very sexy. Stephanie Gray?'

'That's it,' Poppy agreed. 'She's married now. But I'm surprised you even ask. I thought you hadn't liked her.'

The corners of his mouth lifted slightly in amusement. 'Now come on, how could I have helped liking her? Your trouble is, you expect too much – love to order, wedding bells – and after all, she was never *my* guest, was she?'

His stepmother blinked in annoyance. 'Oh, guests! Must we always put everyone into compartments?'

He smiled crookedly. 'That's something I rather thought *you* liked doing . . . I hope you've made plans for entertaining Martyn, anyhow. I'll be out tomorrow, by the way. I haven't had an opportunity up till now for going over to Jindi-yindi, and it's something I must do.'

'Then that'll do for entertainment for a start,' said Poppy promptly. 'You can take Martyn and me with you.'

'Not me.' Martyn almost said it aloud but not quite, it would sound too rude. But how on earth was she going to spend the days now that Jan was not here? And now that she no longer felt she could trust Poppy Diamond who was always inviting girls along for Red's benefit? What on earth had she let herself in for? She squirmed at the thought of how she had arrived complete with new hairdo, pretty clothes, smart travelling case, and she eyed Red covertly through her lashes. He was so sure she was chasing him, but oh no! She would be scared stiff to do *that*. She was willing to bet that anything Bastian had handed out was nothing – but nothing! – compared with what she'd get from this tough man if she ever got tangled up with him.

Meanwhile, he hadn't bothered answering Poppy's suggestion that he should take them with him to Jindi-yindi, wherever that was. He merely said cryptically, 'I thought you didn't like *That Lot*, Poppy.'

Martyn had pushed back her chair. The meal was over, and she badly wanted to escape. She said awkwardly, 'Can I go and help with the washing up?'

Red looked at her quizzically. 'The girls will see to that. Forget about making yourself useful. There's nothing for you to do – not a thing.' His eyes mocked her and she coloured furiously.

'Martyn has a problem,' Poppy interjected quickly. 'A *personal* problem to sort out. Haven't you, Martyn?'

Yes, there was that, she remembered almost with a shock. But she didn't want to air that just now, so she nodded and quickly excused herself. 'Do you mind if I go to bed early? I'm tired, and—' She stopped. *He* was looking at her so – sceptically, so inimically, it was almost more than she could stand. She heard herself say with a rush, 'And I don't particularly want to go to Jindi-yindi tomorrow, thank you very much ... Good night.' She turned away and left the room and found she was on the verge of tears. *Why?* Because she had been made a fool of ... *What* a fool! And she had liked Poppy! But Poppy had been treacherous. It was not really a fair criticism, she knew, but just now it was how she felt – let down. Her pride pricked. Well, she'd get over it.

In her room, the bed had been made up, there were two big fluffy towels, and in a vase on the dressing table some hardy yellow and white and pink wildflowers with prickly leaves.

One thing she didn't have new was pyjamas. Just the thin old striped cotton ones she had worn up the north coast. They were familiar and comforting, and when she'd got into them she felt more herself and she went to stand on the verandah and look out at the dark. It was her lucky night, because a big cheese-coloured moon was just rising over the plains and flooding the land with soft golden light. It was very silent and lonely and just a little bit like looking at the sea when the moon made a path across the waters. When she was a child, she used to think you could walk across it, using the black flecks as stepping stones. Tonight there was no shining path, but there was all that beautiful awesome light spreading out and out, and there were sounds that she didn't know. Not the hush-hush-hush of the waves, but a weird owl's cry, the howling of a wild dog far away, the lowing of cattle. And a sound like a drum, isolated, vibrant.

She wasn't even aware of it when someone came walking along the verandah till Red Diamond's voice said dryly, 'Romantic, isn't it? I can guess the kind of thoughts that are going through your mind.'

'Can you?' she said sarcastically. She had shed a few tears, but they had dried on her cheeks. 'I'll give you a check list, if you like.'

'Spare me that, for God's sake.' He was beside her now, but not too close, and he lit a cigarette. In the glow of the lighter she could see his eyes on her, hard, unamused, assessing. The last because of her schoolgirl pyjamas, she supposed.

She ran her fingers through her hair and said nervily, 'I'd rather you knew than have you guessing. I was just regretting I ever came here. I hadn't an idea your sister wasn't coming — not until I heard Poppy telling you in the car.'

'No? That's a bit hard to believe.'

'It's true,' she flared. 'Ask Poppy. If I *had* known, I

assure you wild horses wouldn't have dragged me here.'

He leaned nonchalantly against the verandah rail, and quite obviously he didn't believe her. Neither, if the truth were told, did she really believe her own words. Because the thought of seeing the outback had been a very tempting one.

'No?' he said cynically.

'*No,*' she repeated furiously.

'All right, don't push it. I won't pile all the blame on you. I know a fair proportion rests with Poppy who made the whole thing possible, and always likes to work things her way.' He paused and drew on his cigarette. 'Nevertheless, if it should enter your head to pester me, now that you *are* here, I'll tell you right now you'd be as well off chasing shadows.'

'Thanks for the advice,' said Martyn angrily. 'But I never chased a man in my life.'

She heard his low laugh. 'You're fooling yourself, aren't you? I've never met a female yet, from six years up, who didn't mark down her quarry and stalk it. Females are natural scalp-hunters, it's instinctive. Just look back a bit at a couple of unexpected encounters we've had, you and I. I'm not flattering myself, but facts are facts, and here you are in the outback, despite everything. Well, it's going to take you rather longer to swim back to the shore this time, but take note, as far as Martyn Verity is concerned, I'm not even as good a bet as Bastian Sinclair — and that's something. I take it he's the focal point of this personal problem you have to sort out, here in the peace and quiet of Diamond Springs, and doubtless with my stepmother fouling up the lines in her own inimitable style.'

Martyn had opened her mouth several times to protest, but he had swept on relentlessly, and now he concluded, 'To get the record really straight, you might like my exact assessment of you—'

Her cheeks burning, she breathed, 'I'd love it — and when I've heard it, maybe you'd like to know what I think of *you*—'

She saw the gleam of his teeth as he smiled grimly. 'Fair enough, I'll buy that. Well, here goes. I see you as a woolly-minded kid who's asking for trouble. I'd say you've probably been horribly spoiled all your life – by everyone. You haven't had to earn your own living, hence you haven't yet discovered that life is real, and that people are real too – very real.' His eyes flicked over her, she could feel it in the almost-dark. 'You're very lovely to look at, and you act sexy in an innocent, pretty little girl way, without knowing just what it is you're inviting. Just don't ever invite me, that's all. You might have a freakish taste for older men, but I don't have one for kids.'

He stopped, and Martyn counted slowly up to ten, and then she told him evenly, 'You've given me good value for an – assessment, haven't you? But don't worry, I'd rather take poison than offer *you* any invitations.' She drew a deep breath and tried to do some quick thinking. 'I wish I had your – your oratorical gifts, but I haven't. I just think of all the men I've ever met – of any age – you're the least likeable, and the one with the nastiest mind. *Full stop.*'

'You've done well,' he said coldly.

They looked at each other through the darkness. Now there was a faint and slightly crooked smile on his mouth, and his eyes looked dark and hard. Martyn's spirits sank down and down. She thought, 'We hate each other.'

He said abruptly, 'I wish to hell you'd listened to me instead of letting my stepmother persuade you into doing something you're going to regret. You must have known the thing about Jan was nothing but a made-up excuse – a very thin story . . . Well, sleep tight, and if there's anything you want, just let out a yell. Someone will hear you, but it won't be me. I sleep on the far side of the house. Goodnight.'

'Goodnight,' she echoed almost inaudibly. She could feel the air vibrating around her, and her whole body felt as if it had been subjected to a very slight but unpleasant electric shock. She thought she would sooner be under Rosalind's feet any day than in the company of that man.

And yet – strangely – she couldn't imagine not having come to Diamond Springs. No matter how thin an excuse helping Jan had been. And that, she was beginning to realize, was possibly only too true. Poppy Diamond had had other things in mind when she had invited her here.

She thought, as she left the verandah rail and went in to bed, that she was glad she hadn't set him right about the nature of her personal problem. He was welcome to think it concerned Bastian Sinclair and to consider her as spoiled and as useless as he liked. She hated him . . .

In the morning, one of the kitchen girls, a pretty aboriginal in a pale blue cotton dress, came barefooted to her room with a cup of tea and a slice of home-baked bread at some hour not long after dawn.

'Brekfus be ready on the v'randah in half a nour, Martyn,' the girl told her cheerfully. Martyn nodded and thanked her. No matter what had happened, she felt great this morning, she had slept well, and now she was eager to see what she could of the outback. She drank the tea, ate the bread and butter, and went along to the bathroom to shower. She saw no one and heard nothing other than muffled sounds from the direction of the kitchen, and when she came back to her room she saw through the long window that opened on to the verandah some stockmen in wide-brimmed hats and checked shirts riding out across the paddock. She didn't suppose Red Diamond would be amongst them, because he was going to Jindi-yindi. And so was Poppy. But she, Martyn, was not. She had told him that last night, and now in the clear light of morning she wished she had not been so hasty.

She got into the soft new off-white jean-style pants that Ros had bought her and a matching short-sleeved jacket. She didn't need to clip her hair back now it was its new

74

length, but she brushed it well and decided to forget about eye make-up. It would probably only aggravate *his* opinion of her as a sex-crazed dolly girl anyhow – and she had half a mind to change out of this gear into a pair of the comfortable old pants she had managed to slip into her case while Ros wasn't looking. She didn't want to give even the vaguest impression of wanting to make an impact on Red, and if that was what Poppy had had in mind when she invited her, then she was sorry, but she wasn't co-operating. If she'd been in some way just a little bit intrigued by Red Diamond, it hadn't counted. She'd come in all good faith to look after Jan – and to think about her own future too, she remembered. It was funny how she could never get her mind seriously fixed on that, mainly because she just couldn't think of one thing she really wanted to do. And how she would hate Red to know *that*! She would probably finish up getting a living-in job minding children. Even if Ros and Dick disapproved, that way she wouldn't be confined indoors all day and she'd have a chance to work on some kind of a children's book ...

At last, somewhat in dread of having to confront her host again, she walked round the verandah to find where breakfast was being celebrated. It wasn't difficult, because of the delicious smell of bacon and toast and coffee – and steak! Her step quickened. She was hungry!

Poppy and Red were at the table already and he stood up and greeted her and pulled out a chair for her as if nothing at all had happened between them the previous night.

'Sleep well?' Poppy asked. 'All ready for a day out?'

Yes, Martyn said, she'd slept well. She didn't answer the other question, and she felt vaguely ill at ease, because of – everything. Not merely because of Red, who had given her a cool and mocking smile.

'Changed your mind about coming to Jindi-yindi?' he asked her casually. He didn't even look at her but reached for the home-made marmalade and gave his attention to his toast. Martyn noticed his hands, broad and dark with strong-looking fingers. He had showered, and his black hair was damp. He wore a dark red shirt with a celadon-green silk neckerchief that looked rather striking. Martyn was saved from answering his question when the little aboriginal girl came softly round the verandah and placed the most enormous plate of steak and eggs and bacon in front of her.

Poppy said, 'Of course she's going to Jindi.' She added, 'We don't go visiting every day of the week out here, Martyn, as you might imagine, so when there's an opportunity it's good sense to take it.'

Martyn smiled and shrugged a little, letting herself be persuaded as abstractedly as if it didn't matter much to her one way or the other, though she had the disagreeable feeling that she had made herself appear childish by her previous perversity.

'Where *is* Jindi-yindi?' she asked as she attacked her breakfast.

'Next door,' Poppy said. 'How far to the homestead, Red?'

'Thirty-three miles,' he said, ignoring Martyn's change of mind. 'Rough miles,' he added. 'We shan't make the journey in a mere hour.'

Martyn made no comment. Inwardly, she felt a little excited at the thought of seeing more of the outback. It wasn't till later – when breakfast was over and she had made final preparations in her room – that she discovered Poppy wasn't coming after all.

Red was waiting in the car and Poppy was standing nearby and smiled apologetically at Martyn when she appeared. 'I'm suffering a reaction from travel and tablets – I think I'd be better staying home today after all Mrs. Hall will bring me up to date on all the local gossip.'

From the car, Red looked at her cryptically. 'You're quite transparent, Poppy, and I assure you the whole manoeuvre's pointless. However, do as you please. But don't believe all you hear, will you? Local gossip's not always very reliable.' He leaned across and opened the door for Martyn, who climbed into the seat beside him with a feeling of slight frustration. It looked as though Poppy was manipulating her!

'Give my regards to the Bowers, Red,' Poppy said brightly.

Her stepson sent her a lopsided smile. 'That Lot? Sure. They'll want to know why you didn't come along ... Well, so long, we'll be home to dinner.'

Another minute and they were alone. Martyn thought it was really crazy. Her first day at Diamond Springs and here she was setting off on a day's outing with the very man she had sworn she would avoid. A man whom she disliked intensely. She had actually told him so! Poppy had worked it this way, and he knew it as well as she did, but he was not going to be allowed to think she was a party to the plan. She would make a point of bringing Bastian's name into the conversation (What conversation? she paused to wonder, because so far there hadn't been any) just as soon as she could. Fortunately she hadn't burnt all her bridges behind her. She'd never confessed to having broken with Bastian, and it shouldn't be all that hard to fabricate a white lie or two – such as that her brother had wanted her to get away for a while so as to sort herself out. That was true enough in its own way, except the sorting out had nothing in the world to do with Bastian ...

She moved a little and tried to concentrate on the outside world – on the red earth covered patchily with tough-looking, not quite green grass, on the ill defined and decidedly bumpy track, on the groups of belahs and wilgas beneath which cattle grazed or lay in the shade. Heat shimmered, and birds flew against the cloudless blue of the sky, and the land seemed very vast, and very empty.

'What's keeping you so quiet?' the man beside her asked so suddenly that she was startled.

'Oh, I was thinking about Richard,' she said quickly.

77

'Richard?' She saw his brow crease and was pleased.

'My brother,' she began, then broke off, discovering that after all it was not so easy to lie. But by saying just those two words she had said enough, because he said at once, 'Your brother's called a halt to it? – suggested you go away and get over your silly infatuation. Is that what you intend to do? I certainly hope so.'

She shrugged, coloured, looked out of the car again at the long lines of fencing. 'I don't know.' She waited to see if he was going to read her another lecture, but he didn't, and after a moment, because it was on her mind, she told him with faint aggressiveness, 'I wouldn't have come today if I'd known Poppy wasn't coming too.'

His brows lifted cynically. 'More protests? But why not? Are you afraid I'll try to seduce you on the way? I assure you I won't.'

Martyn's temper rose. 'My mind doesn't work along those lines. I just meant—' She stopped. What *had* she meant? Was there to be more talk of dislike? Fortunately, at that moment she saw something that distracted her completely – an emu, the first she had ever seen outside a zoo, resting on the ground in the hot sunshine on the other side of the fence beside which the track ran. As the car drew nearer it got to its feet and began to run along beside the fence, watching the car curiously, keeping pace, its long buff and brown feathers flopping and bouncing like thick silky hair.

Martyn was fascinated. Her fingers fairly itched to get hold of a pencil and record that movement. She exclaimed spontaneously, 'Oh, it's beautiful! Those flip-flopping feathers! I've never seen such a sight!' The emu had lost the race now and she twisted round so she could watch it through the back window.

Red said dryly, 'Beautiful's not quite the word I'd have chosen. However, I'm afraid we can't pull up just now. I want to get over to Jindi-yindi. But don't worry, you'll have all the time in the world for bird-watching while you're at Diamond Springs. There aren't all that many

78

other distractions. It's not exactly the centre of the metropolis.'

'I'm not used to city distractions,' she said mildly, though she was seething. 'I'm from the north coast, not from Sydney.'

He didn't comment. He said merely, 'Still, you're going to have lots and lots of time on your hands. If wild life really interests you, you'll be able to watch emus and goannas and cockatoos to your heart's content.'

She made a small grimace. Till you're at screaming point, he could have added, by the sound of his voice. Time on her hands because she shouldn't have come – she wasn't wanted.

Ahead, she could see cattle in a mob, the smoke of a fire, a group of men sitting in the shade of gum trees drinking billy tea, eating slabs of bread. 'Is this Jindi-yindi?' she asked.

'No. We're still on Diamond Springs. Those are my stockmen. We've a muster on, branding the calves. I'm going to stop for a minute.'

He pulled up under a big coolibah and go out. Martyn watched him stride across to the camp and talk for a while to a tall stringy-looking character – his head stock-man, she supposed. Then he looked about him and picked out another stockman who got up from where he was squatting on the ground to come forward with a wide smile. This was an aboriginal, a man with a broad dark, shining face, very white teeth, crinkled-up eyes. She saw Red lay his hand on this other man's shoulder and they talked for a few minutes. Then, with a general gesture of salute, Red had left the stockmen who were now beginning to move towards the horses hobbled beyond the trees.

'Who was that?' she asked impulsively as he got back into the car, and started it up.

He sent her a wordless questioning look.

'The aboriginal,' she said a little impatiently.

'Drummer. One of my best stockmen. His wife's gone

away to town to have another baby – went yesterday with the mail truck. His sister is looking after the other two children.'

Some instinct told Martyn that Red hadn't *needed* to talk to Drummer. He had simply wanted to. She had sensed, as she watched them, an understanding – a sort of comradeship between the two men. She didn't know how or why, and Red had nothing further to say.

Some time later they went through a gate, and he said, 'We're on Jindi-yindi now. They've had a bad time here the last little while – almost ever since they took over, in fact. I don't know if you read in the papers about the rain we had here in the north-west. Diamond Springs was lucky. It did us nothing but good. But Jindi-yindi was hard hit – suffered a lot of flood damage on the far side of the run, lost a lot of stock and had miles of fencing washed away. These things can be disastrous for a man on the land – they can ruin him.'

Martyn listened. She had already heard Poppy Diamond say there was a 'hex' on Jindi-yindi, and she had the feeling that Poppy didn't much like the folk there – That Lot. Martyn was sorry they'd had a bad time. Here, you certainly couldn't notice it. There was plenty of pasture, and there were stands of trees that made pleasant shade or sheltered a dam. The cattle she saw looked sleek and well fed.

Red said presently, 'They need capital to buy more stock and to repair their fencing.' He said it musingly almost as though he had forgotten she was there, and quite suddenly she wondered about the people on Jindi-yindi. Were they young people? Or were they old folks?

It wasn't long before she found out.

# CHAPTER FIVE

THE usual thick grove of trees that shelter a homestead appeared, and in minutes they had pulled up outside the garden.

'We're not expected,' Red said, climbing out of the car, while Martyn opened her own door and slid out quickly, smoothing down her new pants. She felt the air hot on her head and arms. At the coast, the air was moist and salty, here it felt very dry, but clean and good. As she moved round the car to join Red he told her, 'You should wear sun glasses. Those beautiful blue eyes will be ruined and you'll look old before your time if you don't watch out.'

'Who cares? Anyhow, I won't be here all that long. At home I never wore sunglasses, not even on the beach. Stan said healthy eyes could stand strong sunlight – and read small print by candlelight as well. And *his* mother—' She stopped because he was staring at her with a sort of quizzical amusement.

'Stan?'

She flushed. They had begun to walk towards the house. 'My father.'

'Oh. He died recently, you said.'

'Yes.' She averted her face. He had spoken gently, and if she wasn't careful, she still cried over Stan.

Ahead of them, the screen door opened and a girl appeared at the top of the steps. She called out delightedly, '*Red*!' and came quickly down towards them – almost into his arms, her hands outstretched. He took them in his.

'Surprised to see me, Fay? I thought it was time to pay my respects. Is David about?'

'He's out on the run somewhere,' Fay said. Red released her hands and reached out towards Martyn almost absentmindedly.

'This is Martyn Verity. Martyn – Fay Bower.'

Martyn said, 'Hello,' and was aware at once that the other girl was wondering who on earth she was. Red's introduction had been the briefest possible, but after a bright, 'Hello,' she put her arm through his and invited, 'Come in and have a nice cold beer.'

Red released his arm. 'Sorry, not now, Fay. Lunch later, if Maude can manage it? Right now, I want to catch up with David.'

'Oh. Then I *think* he went over to see how the fencing was going. You'll need to drive. Shall I—'

'You and Martyn stay here – get to know each other,' he added, and to Martyn it seemed his eyes glinted. 'I know my way about. Besides, you'll have to do some planning with unexpected guests to lunch. Poppy sent her regards, by the way – she came home yesterday, brought Martyn with her.' He nodded briskly and moved back to the car leaving the two girls together.

While the conversation in which she had taken no part had been going on, Martyn had taken in a few facts about Fay Bower. She was an attractive-looking girl – young woman, rather – with brown hair that had a smoky sheen on it. Martyn put her age at about twenty-eight. Her eyes were the colour of champagne, and she was tall, slim, straight, and lightly tanned – not nearly so brown as Martyn. Even though she hadn't been expecting visitors, she looked immaculate in pale blue cotton slacks with a sleeveless ribbed matching top. Martyn was glad after all that she hadn't sneaked back and got into her old clothes. She'd have felt at a distinct disadvantage. As it was, she somehow didn't feel very much at her ease.

Both of them watched the car move off, and then Fay looked at Martyn. In fact, she looked her over – from head to foot, and very rapidly. She said briskly, 'Come on in and I'll see about some cold drinks.'

Martyn followed her on to the verandah, Fay indicated a chair and disappeared. Not very hospitable, Martyn decided. She could have invited her out to the kitchen. She looked around her. There were half a dozen cane chairs, a small round table, a couple of ceiling lights. Everything was a little dilapidated, and the floor, after the clean shining polished verandah floor at Diamond Springs, needed not only a bit of polish but a sweeping and a good scrubbing as well. The Bowers certainly couldn't have as good house staff as they had at Diamond Springs, Martyn thought, as she sat down and waited for Fay to rejoin her.

She waited a long time with nothing to do but stare out at the garden which, though you couldn't say it was overgrown, was certainly not very well tended. She thought of what Red had said about the flood damage, and how the property needed capital, and she supposed that their finances had been affected badly and that possibly they'd had to cut down on staff. Presently her thoughts wandered to the emu she and Red had seen, and she wished she'd brought éven a small sketch pad along with her today. She could have done a sketch from memory. Bastian – and Mrs. Turner too – had always said it was a very valuable exercise. It taught you a lot about observation, and made you take in more next time you had an opportunity. But she didn't even have a scrap of paper with her – she hadn't brought a handbag. So – time on her hands. Sounds, voices, from somewhere inside the house. It looked as if Fay had forgotten her and was doing something about lunch.

Someone else joined her on the verandah before Fay did. A man. She saw him come along the gravel path, climb the steps, push the door open and let it swing shut behind him. Then he stood staring.

'Hello!' He all but whistled as he said it. Martyn had heard Hello said with exactly that intonation many times before – usually on the beach. She never took any notice because she'd learned it was a sort of opening gambit, and before you knew where you were, you had someone on your hands that you didn't want to know. On the beach, she never even bothered looking up, but here – well, she was on the verandah of the Jindi-yindi homestead, and she had to be polite, so she smiled, and didn't turn away. She saw a very good-looking man in a long-sleeved dull green shirt, narrow cord trousers, and tan boots that had only a light film of dust on them. He had the film star good looks that Red Diamond lacked. Thick burnished brown hair, even features, a square forehead; good teeth that showed because he was smiling at her – good, but not as white as Red's, she noted automatically. Age? About old enough to be Fay Bower's husband. Of course! That was who he was, she thought with an odd sort of relief. And Red must have missed him.

She stayed where she was and he came towards her. It was then she noticed his eyes – champagne-coloured, and they licked her over in one swipe and swallowed her whole.

No, not Fay's husband. Her brother.

He had come to a dead stop in front of her when Fay appeared carrying a tray, glasses, a jug of fruit juice in which ice tinkled.

'Oh, David, I heard the door. You didn't see Red?'

As if it needed an effort, he shifted his eyes from Martyn. 'No. Should I have? Aren't you going to introduce us? We haven't got beyond just – looking – yet.'

Fay deposited the tray on the table. 'Sorry. This is—' She stopped, she'd forgotten of course, and Martyn said obligingly, 'Martyn Verity.'

'She's a guest at Diamond Springs, came over with Poppy,' Fay said, and added somewhat belatedly, 'My brother David.'

He looked at Martyn and raised one eyebrow. 'With Poppy? Not with Red?'

Martyn felt irritated all of a sudden. She hated that instant, insincere, flattery-by-implication thing, and wondered what he'd think if she said – as she'd heard girls say on the beach, at club dances – 'Oh, go and get lost!'

She said politely, 'I came with Poppy, Red came earlier. I know him, of course. I met him at his sister's house.'

There was a tiny silence, then Fay, who was pouring the drinks, said brightly, 'Really? So you got yourself an invitation. Well, I suppose it wasn't hard. Poppy likes to bring – *eligible* girls out to Diamond Springs. She thinks it's good for Red.' She handed a glass of fruit drink carelessly to Martyn, who immediately had to wipe a few spilled drops from her white pants with a tissue from her pocket. She said evenly, as Fay passed a glass to David, 'And isn't it good for him?'

She looked at the other girl, and sipped her drink. She was wondering why she hadn't dropped dead the way Fay was looking at her. So Red was *her* property. Was that the message? She rather thought it was. Well, she was welcome to him.

Fay said in a clipped voice, 'Red can manage his own life. He doesn't need an interfering stepmother around trying to push him some way he doesn't want to go.'

'I don't think anyone could do that,' said Martyn, a little surprised at her own coolness. 'Do you?'

Fay didn't answer. She said, 'What's the news of Jan? Or aren't you up to date with that? She'd got herself into a very nasty psychological mess last time I heard.'

'You'd better ask Red about it,' Martyn said carefully. 'But I don't really think Jan is in a mess at all.'

'Then you don't know a thing,' Fay said. 'Well, I'd better get back to the kitchen.' She turned to David. 'I shall never understand why Lewis had blacks working in the kitchen for him. If I wasn't sure of being out of this place before long, I think I'd strangle Maude with my bare hands. Two extra people for lunch and she expects me to work out every minute detail. It's like having an imbecile – or a monkey – working for you!'

'Calm down,' said David. 'Just remember she started here as a girl under old Annie Bower's rule, and you'll forgive her everything.'

Fay gave him an angry glare and disappeared inside the house, and he grinned and sat down on the arm of a chair he had moved in Martyn's direction.

85

There was silence for a moment and she moved uneasily, knowing she was being looked at again, and wishing, rather illogically, that Red would come back. Wishing too that she *had* put her old jeans on today – David Bower might not have been so fixated then. She leaned back in her chair, raised her glass of fruit drink and looked cautiously over it at the staring and oh, so handsome David.

'Has your family lived here for a long time, Mr. Bower?' she asked, like a polite schoolgirl.

'*David*,' he insisted. 'I'm not that old ... No, the Bowers haven't lived at Jindi-yindi so long, actually. If you want the history – Annie Bower's father, Old Man Richardson, was the first owner, and as Annie was the only child, she inherited the place when he died, and ran it like a man. She'd always worked with the old boy – was out on the run with him every day from the moment she could sit a horse. She married a Bower – Charles, who was my great-uncle. He wasn't a countryman, so she kept on running the property – she was one of these frightfully forceful females, and poor old Charles opted out at forty – was kicked to death by a wild horse or something. They had a son Lewis, and that was the beginning of the Bower rule, except that Lewis was never allowed to reign, his mother did it all for him. And that,' he finished with a wry grimace, 'is why the old place was a bit of a shambles when it came to me and Fay. After Annie died, Lewis didn't know if he was on his head or his feet, he wasn't capable of organizing a fowlyard, let alone a cattle run, and the first thing he did was sack anyone who knew more than he did. Which left him with a few half-trained aboriginal stockmen.'

'And then you had the flood,' Martyn prompted. She liked him a lot better when he was being – even slightly – informative and amusing, instead of acting the Romeo.

'Yes. Who told you about that?'

'Red, of course.'

'Of course,' he repeated. 'So I suppose you know all

86

about Fay and me as well.'

'No.' She looked at him directly. 'I didn't even know either of you existed till I met you.'

'No? Well, maybe I'm not worth a mention, but I'd have thought Red would have had something to say about Fay,' said David, narrowing his eyes.

'Why?' If you want to know something, the best way to find out is to be blunt and to ask, Stan had always said. But David wasn't putting it into words.

'I'll give you three guesses,' he said, and then he smiled and reached for her glass. 'More?'

So he meant that Fay and Red were interested in each other. Somehow, the information sent a little electric shock up and down Martyn's spine.

'Now tell me about yourself,' he insisted when she had refused another drink. 'What lured you away from the city and brought you to the outback? Holiday and nowhere to go?'

She widened her eyes. 'Something like that. And the outback is special, isn't it?'

'Is it? What about Red? You wouldn't be the first girl to come here on a visit on his account, you know.'

'I'm sure I wouldn't,' Martyn agreed, a little bored at having her motives made suspect. 'But as a matter of fact, I agreed to come because Jan was supposed to be coming, and Poppy wanted me to keep her company and help her with swimming, as a kind of remedial exercise.'

'I see. The poor girl did some damage to her leg, didn't she? But you came, and she didn't, so I don't quite get it.'

Martyn was exasperated. Was she supposed to have come because she was madly in love with Red Diamond? It was absurd to take it almost for granted that every girl who came here had fallen in love with a tough-looking character who appeared to have no heart. He wasn't at all the sort of man Ros had had in mind, she was sure, when she had hoped that Martyn would meet up with some uncomplicated outdoor type.

Meanwhile, however, for what reason she didn't know, David had evidently decided to believe her guiltless and to tell her, 'Well then, there's no reason why you and I shouldn't get together now and again since you're here, is there?'

She flushed, but it was mainly with annoyance. She just didn't like his tactics, she didn't understand them. She hadn't found a suitable answer when Red himself arrived back, and the twosome was split up.

Lunch was a very plain salad with cold beef and glasses of beer – which Martyn didn't take, so was given more fruit drink. They ate on the side verandah, and the table was already laid when Fay came to say it was ready. Martyn didn't catch even a glimpse of the bothersome Maude, but she had a break from David's concentrated attention while the talk was of Jan and her mended engagement, and of the fact that the fencing repairs had been started. She picked up the point that Red had recommended a certain contractor, but that David had been lucky and got on to someone who would do the job thirty per cent cheaper.

The reason David hadn't been where Red had expected was because he had been exercising a new mount he'd bought, a thoroughbred named Regal.

'Cost me a packet,' said David, 'but a good horse is something I can't live without. That's one thing I've missed since Fay and I moved out here. Nothing on the place but stock horses and most of them are only half broken. I don't think there's a good horse breaker on the property either – I daresay old Annie used to do that part of the work herself, I wouldn't put it past her,' he added half jokingly. 'By the way, Red, I was going to ask your advice about buying some store cattle that are being brought down to the sales from Queensland. Should I take a look at them?'

'I'd say so. In fact, I'd intended to mention it to you. It would be a good move. You've got plenty of feed here.'

'Great,' nodded David. 'Feel like coming along with me?'

Red picked up his half empty beer glass. 'Sorry, I shan't be buying, so I can't spare the time,' he said a trifle tersely. 'But you're quite capable of making your own decisions – your own judgments.'

David shrugged. 'I'm not as well acquainted with inland cattle as you are. Still, if it's not convenient— And of course you have a guest. Eh, Martyn?'

Martyn, taken by surprise at being brought so suddenly on stage and into the limelight, blushed scarlet. The Bowers, both brother and sister, were concentrating their attention on her, and she waited for Red to correct David to say, 'Martyn's Poppy's guest.' But he didn't. He said blandly, 'That's right ... But I'm sure you can manage without me, David. Well, I'll let you get back to work. I know you're busy and I have plenty to do myself. We must be on our way.'

Fay said almost sharply, 'I'm disappointed. I thought I was going to have some company for a change. What about Sunday, Red?'

'Come over and we'll organize a picnic,' he said laconically. He pushed back his chair and got to his feet and the others did likewise. 'Bring your bathing gear and we'll go to the swimming hole and maybe have a campfire afterwards. We have a swimmer in our midst, by the way, so you'll have to be on your mettle, Fay.'

Fay looked at Martyn and in her champagne-coloured eyes dislike was very thinly veiled. Martyn was aware of it behind the sparkling smile.

'I should have guessed you're a swimmer – that accounts for those lovely strong-looking shoulders.'

It was a decidedly backhanded compliment, but David cupped a hand over one of Martyn's shoulders at once, and with difficulty she stopped herself from pulling away. She didn't like being handled so casually, so familiarly, by someone she didn't know. He said, 'Martyn's a perfect physical specimen.'

She bit her lip. How was she supposed to react to that? It was so – dopey, so obvious. Fay looked at Red and Red looked as if he simply hadn't heard. He said, 'Come along, Martyn, fetch your jacket or whatever else you've left lying about—'

'My jacket's in the car,' she said quickly. 'And I haven't anything else.'

'No handbag? No make-up kit?'

'No,' she said flatly.

On the way out to the car, while she and David went ahead down the verandah steps, the other two followed slowly behind, and when Martyn paused by the car and looked back, Fay had her hand on Red's chest and was looking up into his face. A brief flash of unexpected emotion burned through Martyn like a flame and left her – aching. Incomprehensibly. So he was human – susceptible – despite the fact he looked so tough. Today even his hair looked wild, and his shoulders – they were just that little bit too broad for true masculine good looks. The man beside her – David Bower – was lighter, lither, more civilized in every way. More easily comprehensible too. And yet – a mark in Red's favour – David was not as straight, as blunt and sincere. He was a flatterer, he had a way with him. And Martyn was very well aware of it. So why—?

Her thoughts became indistinct, blurred. She had no idea what David was saying to her, though she didn't realize it for seconds. She was watching Red intently. He was so physically fit, but not in the least like the swimmers she had known. Nor was he like the fishermen who went out to sea from the small north coast town where she had been born and bred. There was a wild, burning, steely sort of toughness about him that could never be broken. There would be no tenderness in him, not like there had been in Stan, who had so often tucked her in at night, been gentle and understanding when she had problems at school, or when she was feeling depressed or out of sorts. And even when Red looked down at Fay as he was doing now, he did it in an intent kind of way, not in a tender way. Unless there was a hidden softness in his eyes that only Fay could see . . .

He came to join her at last, and at last the good-byes had been said and they were on their way. They didn't speak to each other for minutes, and then he said abruptly and without looking at her, 'Don't be flattered too much by David's attentions. I know you go for older men, but I wouldn't recommend you should talk yourself into a love affair with David Bower while you're here.'

She felt herself bristle with hostility. 'Why not? I imagine at least he's a gentleman. And anyhow, it was he who was doing the chasing, in case you hadn't noticed — not me.'

His brows tilted. 'Admittedly that's a change,' he allowed, infuriatingly. 'But all the same, I'll guarantee you gave him the green light. The woman always does. Perhaps you're too young to be fully conscious of your own wiles yet, but it's a fact.'

'You're — cynical,' she said. 'Hard.'

'As diamonds,' he agreed. 'I've a reputation in the outback, and that's it.' He turned to look at her quickly and she felt the fire of his grey eyes, and she wondered nervily if he thought she had ever given *him* the green light. She had no idea what to expect of him or what he might suspect of her, and it was maddening and disconcerting. Then suddenly he dropped personalities as the car bucked a little.

'This car's running like a pig. I'll have to get Harry to give it an overhaul.'

Martyn sank back in the seat, relieved to be forgotten.

She went to bed early after dinner that night, but she lay awake in the darkness for a long time. From towards the end of the verandah she could hear voices, and soon, because she had sharp ears and she was sleepless, she began to pick up what was being said. She listened quite deliberately. In real life, people don't block their ears and hurry away too soon – if they're interested. And Martyn was interested. Besides, she was in bed where she had every right to be, and they must know she was there. Because her light was out, they no doubt thought she was asleep, but if they didn't want her to hear, then they should have talked somewhere else.

Poppy said, 'I really don't know why you bother with That Lot, Tancred. They're rubbish – weaklings. Not like the Richardsons. Why, Lewis was so ineffective he was the joke of the district.'

Silence.

Then Poppy again. 'I sometimes wonder if Fay would have been so charming to Lewis if she'd known just how far the place had gone down the drain . . . Of course they want your help, and it would suit David very well to have you part of the show. In my opinion, he's a fool – even though a persuasive one. He's the type who lets other people do the work while he takes all the credit.'

'Do you call that being a fool?' Red asked dryly. 'In any case, you've got the bull by the tail. From my angle, Jindi-yindi's no more than a side issue. I'll admit I don't like to see a good property going to seed, and I'm convinced that all that's needed is good management and a bit of capital.'

'And if you're going to provide both,' she retorted heatedly, 'then Diamond Springs will be the loser. You're playing right into their hands.'

'Oh, for God's sake, Poppy, try to be a bit realistic. I know exactly what I'm doing. I don't need your personal opinions or your interference, however well-meaning they may be. Anything I do, you can be sure I do it because that's what I want to do. I like Fay – she's intelligent, mature and healthy – and those are three of the attributes an outback man should look for in a wife.'

'You talk like a man without a heart,' said Poppy. 'You always have. But this time you're being reckless as well, trying to mix – love – with business. Bad business at that, in my opinion. There are plenty of girls in the world.

Why should you have to choose someone like Fay Bower? Oh, when I think of all the other girls – nice girls – you've loved and dropped—'

'Loved? When you're young, love's nothing but a game. And I'm sorry, but I've never worn rose-coloured glasses in my life.'

That was all Martyn heard, lying wide-eyed in the dark. The voices faded and she turned on her side. Love's a game – when you're young. How wrong he was! Martyn was positive she took love twice as seriously as he appeared to. He was thinking of marrying Fay Bower – that was clear. Not because he loved her, but because she had the attributes! And because he was interested in Jindi-yindi? Somehow, the thought made Martyn feel sick. Why on earth was that? She turned on her other side and resolutely refused to think of that moment when she had looked at him and Fay Bower standing together and a flame had burned through her heart ...

Martyn's knowledge of the Jindi-yindi set-up was expanded a little next day by Poppy, who chose that day also to reveal the contents of the large suitcases she had brought from Sydney. Curtain material.

'I'm going to make new curtains for all the bedrooms,' she said firmly. 'I don't live here any more, I only visit – I'd drive Red bananas if I stayed for long – but I love the place, and it does need a woman's interest to keep it the way it is. You know what I mean? Or am I crazy thinking there's something special about this old homestead?'

Martyn shook her head, thinking of the feelings she had had at Jindi-yindi. They were on a side verandah where vines made a cool screen against the heat of the day, for outside the sun was blazingly hot. Martyn had risen fairly early, but Red had already gone out on the run – for which she was thankful – and she had break-fasted alone with Poppy. 'Jindi-yindi has a kind of – neglected look,' she said tentatively after a moment.

Poppy had taken tape-measure and scissors from the drawer of a big table and was spreading out a length of soft pastel green material, and was looking very business-like and determined. Now she looked up briefly.

'Did Tancred tell you about Jindi-yindi?'

'No. But I gathered from David that it had been left to him and Fay by some sort of a relation.'

'That's right – Lewis Bower. He was in love with Fay, and although he was about thirty years her senior, she played him along. It may sound catty to say so, but it's true.'

'But she didn't marry him?'

'No. His mother, old Annie Bower, wouldn't hear of second or third cousins marrying, and Lewis always complied with her wishes. But of course he left the property to Fay and her brother – which was exactly what she'd hoped for. They've had to raise a mortgage to pay the death duties and they're in a bit of a financial fix at the moment, but Fay has plans for remedying *that.*'

Martyn didn't ask how, she already knew. And after a second she changed the subject and asked if she could help with the curtain-making.

'No, no.' Poppy was quite emphatic. 'You're here to amuse yourself, not to be my offsider. Tomorrow we must persuade Red to take you out on the run, but today, why don't you take a ride, or go down to the swimming pool? Goodness knows, it's hot enough.'

That was true, and finally, feeling completely useless, Martyn took herself off and spent a good part of the day at the river. The swimming pool there was wide and deep, its banks fringed with acacias, and willows and tall red river gums, and she swam and wallowed lazily for a long time, then lay on her towel in the shade. She didn't know why, but she felt vaguely troubled and on edge. She thought about her future, and what would happen when she went back to Sydney. 'Three weeks will go in a flash,' she told herself. 'And I shan't be seeing much of *him.*' Red Diamond, who was planning to marry a girl who possessed at least three of the attributes required of an outback wife. Intelligence, maturity, and health. Health was the only point Martyn would score, and she wasn't part owner of a neighbouring cattle station either, however run-down. Appalled at the irrational quality of her unexpected thought, she got up and dived into the water again.

When she walked back to the homestead it was not long before sundown and Red had just come in.

He said without preamble, merely flicking his eyes over her suntanned face, completely devoid of make-up, 'Sling your swimming things down somewhere and I'll take you out to the far waterhole to see the birds. I suppose you ride?'

Protests rose in her throat – 'I don't want you to think you have to entertain me' – but they were never uttered, he simply didn't give her an opportunity. He hadn't, in fact, paused as he spoke to her, but kept on walking towards the house, and he tossed back over his shoulder, 'Be down at the horse paddock in five minutes' time.'

She was there, and she refused to think why. She hadn't ever done any riding, but he helped her up into the saddle and she took the reins in her hands and felt her heart beating fast. As they started off, he sent her a cynical glance.

'You don't ride, do you, mermaid? Only sea-horses and the surf. Well, you won't come to any harm, I'll look after you.'

She didn't need his reassurance, but didn't say so. She felt safe enough riding slowly along the track, over the paddock and through a grove of smallish twisted trees. It was the end of the day and the sun was sliding fast down to the horizon – a flat, limitless horizon – through a paling, cloudless sky. The air had assumed a peculiar clarity and every hanging leaf, every blade of grass seemed sharply outlined. And he, riding a little ahead of her just now – hatless, his dark hair burnished – he was sharply etched too. Red Diamond. Inside her was an unanalysable feeling of elation, topped with a kind of

95

cynical amazement at herself and her own unpre-
dictableness.

The waterhole, when they reached it, was silver-grey
like his eyes, and then, slowly and quite fascinatingly, it
turned rose and finally brilliant crimson. They left their
horses and she followed him, all eyes, to stand entranced
as a myriad birds began to fly in – from the trees, from the
skies, from nowhere. Tiny jewel-coloured budgerigars
floated down like a storm of bright coloured leaves; noisy
white cockatoos, brilliant parrots alighted on the water in
swarms; there was a cloud of finches, and in the shallows
long-legged birds waded.

Martyn watched till her eyes almost fell out and at last
she turned to the man at her side and said on a long soft
breath – 'Oh!' Bastian would have said, 'What about a
few quick sketches?' but this man wasn't Bastian, he was
Red Diamond. His heavy eyebrows curved up and then
descended and his unnervingly brilliant eyes glinted at
her. He reached in his pocket for cigarettes, and suddenly
she somehow knew that while she had watched the birds,
he had been watching her. Gaping, infantile, she supposed.

He said casually, 'Now you're acting like the kid you
really are.'

'I'm not a kid,' she said with dignity. 'I'm nineteen.
These days, that's quite an age, and I assure you I'm well
clued up. I'm not the – neophyte you like to picture
me.'

He bit on his full lower lip for a second. 'Well, well,
that's quite a word, isn't it? What are you trying to tell
me? That you know it all and can handle it?'

There was carmine light reflected on his face and she
saw it burn like fire in his eyes as he suddenly whipped
around and took hold of her shoulders. Then with a
tricky movement he jerked her so that her head was flung
back and she found herself staring up into his face, momentarily paralysed, her blue eyes wide, unblinking.
Inside she could feel herself quaking and she was afraid.

If he should kiss her now – if that mouth, long, curving, deadly, with its tilted corners, its sensual lower lip, should touch her own – if he should press her to him savagely as Bastian had done, force her lips apart – then she would die.

Her gaze, that had become riveted on his lips, lifted slowly to his eyes and she suffered the full force of their dagger-bright regard.

He said, his voice so low that she could scarcely hear the words, 'Are you aware that you're inviting me to kiss you – to make love to you, Martyn Verity?'

She stared dumbly. Her mind seemed incapable of operating, but she moved her head almost imperceptibly in a gesture of denial. She saw the darkness of his jaw – he was a man who needed to shave twice a day – and was very much aware of his sheer physical strength, his broadness, his maleness – and of the fingers that tightened and tightened on her shoulders until she could have screamed with the pain of it. His face moved closer to her own, his features blurred, his eyes dazzled her. She could scarcely breathe. And then—

'Because,' he said, his voice now crisp and clipped, 'I'm not going to. Do you understand – mermaid?'

Anticlimax! She felt herself relax, collapse, and for a second she wanted to laugh hysterically. Her tongue came out to moisten her lips, and unexpectedly her eyes were swimming with tears.

He moved one hand away from her shoulder. A finger, not long and slim and artistic like Bastian's, but strong and masculine, sketched a brief line beneath each of her lower lids as he flicked her fallen tears away.

'What do these signify? Disappointment?'

'Relief,' she said huskily, trying to rally.

'You're frightened of me?'

'I could be,' she said, and tried to smile. She pushed back her hair with a hand that trembled, though she hoped he wasn't aware of it. The birds had gone, the water was still, and the sky colourless.

'I wonder why,' he said, close to her hair.

She didn't answer.

'Another evening,' he pursued, 'you'll be able to come on your own.'

'It will be preferable,' she said, her self-control coming back. She moved away from him abruptly and sought the horses that stood beneath the trees. It was maddening to have to allow him to help her to mount, but nerves had given her *some* courage and she was very quickly off and away, letting her horse have its head and take her back to the homestead.

She didn't shower before dinner that night. Instead, she lay flat on her back on her bed for twenty minutes, her mind a determined blank – or as near as she could make it. No matter what she wanted or didn't want, there seemed to be *something* between her and Red Diamond – something struggling underground, trying to get through to the surface. She couldn't think why he had touched her as he had, and she wished desperately that he had not. She hadn't invited anything – she wouldn't dare. She could feel her shoulders still tingling from his grip.

She had all but gone to sleep when the sound of voices, the awareness of light falling slantingly across the verandah outside her room, made her struggle up and switch on the bedside light. She was sticky with perspiration and wished she had showered after all, but a glance at her watch showed her it was too late. If she hadn't been hungry, she might have decided to go without dinner. Though what was she afraid of, for heaven's sake?

Like a stone, the thought of Fay Bower dropped into her mind. 'I needn't be afraid of him,' she told herself firmly but indecipherably.

She opened the wardrobe door and looked at the two pretty special occasion dresses Ros had insisted on providing her with. Her hand already outstretched, she withdrew it. She got into pants and blouse instead. She whisked a brush through her tangled hair and saw her eyes staring back at her, like sapphires, from the mirror.

Something had happened in her life, something to do with Red Diamond, who had no intention of either kissing her or making love to her. But who was planning a cold-blooded marriage with that girl at Jindi-yindi.

After dinner Poppy excused herself and went to the kitchen, murmuring that there was something she had to see Mrs. Hall about. She didn't come back and presently Red rose and disappeared, presumably to the office, underlining the fact, Martyn reflected, that she wasn't *his* guest. Left alone, she made a rueful face, then went to her room to fetch pen and drawing block. She settled herself at a small table outside her room and began to sketch from memory some of the birds she had seen that evening, and to think of her so far non-existent children's story book. As her absorption grew, she relaxed. The outdoor girl slipped into her role of artist, of dreamer – who saw the world through the glisten of her own lashes, saw rainbow, diamond colours as she recreated that vision of the birds flying down, drinking, rising again, feathery shadows against a brilliant sky.

It was only a dawning consciousness of the utter silence of the bush that eventually aroused her, and she sat listening, intensely aware that the one sound that had been part of her life since its very beginning – the sound of the sea – was absent. She felt a surge of loneliness and homesickness and longing for Stan swept over her in a wave.

# CHAPTER SIX

WITHOUT making a thing of it, Martyn simply didn't take up Poppy's idea that she should go out on the run with Red next day – or that she should ride out to the muster later on. Red hadn't invited her to come, and besides, there was Fay – the Bower Bird, as Poppy called her. She got into shorts and long socks, and since her help wasn't required around the homestead, wandered around past the men's quarters. There she came on some little aboriginal children playing in the dust in the shade of the pepper trees. She stood watching them for a while before she wandered on, and in the afternoon she came back again, this time equipped with small sketch pad and fibre-tipped pen.

The kids were there again, there were some noisy clownish galahs in the trees above and there was a puppy – Noosa, they called her, yellowish, skinny, with a tail that wagged like fury. The pup was chewing on a raw carrot but rushed eagerly to greet Martyn as if she were an old friend. She discovered the children belonged to Drummer, the stockman to whom Red had spoken the day they drove to Jindi-yindi. They were being looked after in their mother's absence by Elsey, a large-eyed, skinny-legged aboriginal girl in a pink cotton dress, who appeared from a small verandahed bungalow to make sure they were not getting up to any mischief.

Martyn soon made friends with the children – two small girls – and did some drawings of them. She had never before in her life had the opportunity to draw little aboriginal children with dark shining eyes and shy smiles, and it was an adventure and a delight, and she did a couple of drawings of the pup as well, to amuse them.

She had stuffed sketch pad and pen into her hip pocket

and started back up the dusty track for home when she encountered Red.

'What have you been up to?' he asked, his eyes flicking over her disparagingly in her shorts and socks.

'I've been talking to some children,' she said, half defiant and thankful he hadn't caught her out drawing. 'Shedding my pseudo-sophistication. Finding my own level with the three- and four-year-olds.'

His face stayed expressionless. 'Drummer's children,' he commented. 'Their aunt's looking after them. Elsey's never worked at the homestead – she's likely to go walk-about on the spur of the moment.'

Despite herself, Martyn was intrigued. They were walking back to the homestead together, and she asked, 'What if she should go now? What would happen to the children?'

'She'd take them with her. They'd be all right.'

Later, in the sitting-room, he complained half seriously to Poppy, 'You're not looking after your guest very well. She's been down making friends with Drummer's children.'

'What's wrong with that? Martyn's free to come and go as she pleases.' They were about to have pre-dinner drinks, but Poppy was still busily hand hemming some of the curtains she had been making, light pretty things.

Red sent Martyn a mocking glance. 'She's free within limits,' he allowed. He picked up a corner of the fabric and rubbed it between finger and thumb. 'If these are for here – we don't need new curtains, you know.'

'That's what you think,' contradicted Poppy. 'I got the girls to wash some of the old ones out today – they've fallen to pieces.'

'It's that infernal washing machine,' he said with a frown. He had poured the drinks and handed one to Martyn absentmindedly, and she watched him covertly as he moved and relaxed in a chair – showered, newly shaved and very much the master of the house. The room suited him. It wasn't completely masculine, there were flowers, copper candlesticks, furniture that was solid and unpretentious and that Martyn suspected had been there for ever; for ever, in Australia, not being all that long by world standards, but still, long in the eyes of a girl brought up in the residence of a small town swimming baths. 'It's as bad as a mincing machine,' Red said.

Poppy laughed aloud. 'And you're as bad as your father, Tancred. The fuss he made when we had that washer installed! The old ways were good enough for Diamond Springs! Well, it's a good machine – still is – but as a matter of fact, the girls did those curtains by hand, they're scared of the machine.'

He looked at her and shrugged his broad shoulders. He wasn't really interested, in fact he was irritated by these domestic details. Martyn sensed it, yet Poppy would be quite content to prattle on all evening about curtains, washing machines, the girls who helped in the house. Through her eyelashes, Martyn caught Red's regard, and it sent strange impulses vibrating through her veins.

Poppy said complacently, 'Anyhow, if I make curtains now, it might save someone the trouble later on ... Does Fay like sewing – decorating?' she added innocently.

He made an impatient movement. 'I haven't the least idea. It's hardly relevant.'

Poppy raised her eyes and her eyebrows as if he were hopeless. 'I'm sure *you* sew, Martyn,' she persisted.

Red got to his feet abruptly. 'Mermaids don't sew. And dinner is ready,' he said, putting an end to the conversation ...

Next day was the day Martyn discovered the emus. She had decided to take a ride, and Bob, down at the saddling yards, got a horse ready for her and helped her to mount. She rode off along a track that followed a fence, on the principle that if she followed that, there should be no difficulty in finding her way home again, though as a matter of fact she was a girl with a very well developed sense of direction. She had gone a good long way, without finding it particularly entertaining as both fence and track seemed to continue on for ever. She was beginning to feel more at ease with the horse and wondered if she might possibly see any of the stockmen, or even a mob of cattle, for after all this was a cattle station, and was looking about her with this hope in mind, when she saw an emu appear from a stand of trees some way ahead. Tall, long-legged, it strode confidently along, its feathers flowing back, its small head, on the end of the extraordinarily long neck, turning curiously this way and that.

She had reined in the minute she saw it and it appeared to be quite unaware of her presence as it strode along and finally disappeared into another clump of trees. She was deciding whether or not to pursue it when to her surprise another emu appeared, this one accompanied by five small chicks that immediately put her in mind of aboriginal drawings, with their egg-shaped bodies softly striped in cream and brown, and their little curved necks. They reached scarcely higher than half-way up to the scaly knees of the adult whom Martyn took (quite mistakenly, she discovered later) to be their mother.

The little group followed the route the other bird had taken, but travelled more slowly because of the smallness of the chicks. Reaching the edge of the far group of trees, they loitered to pick around in the dirt and the bark, looking for seeds and insects. Martyn urged her horse quietly forward, but the adult became aware of her. It grunted, emitted a hissing sound and turned to face her aggressively, ready to defend its young. She pulled up at once, and the next minute the chicks had been herded out of sight amongst the trees.

She felt a great deal of pleasure in what she had seen, and determined to do some drawings. More, as she continued her ride, the idea came into her head that she could do a book about two little children lost in the bush – one white, the other a little aboriginal. They would be found by an emu and taken into its care with its other young. That would be great! She felt full of enthusiasm.

They could encounter other birds – comical galahs, chattering parrots, those surprised-looking white cockatoos with the sulphur crests, laughing kookaburras. And maybe a goanna or two and a kangaroo.

She swore to herself that in future she would always carry a sketchbook with her, and when she came out riding she would have a definite purpose. It looked as though she had at last found a rather more rational way of filling in her days.

Then it was Sunday, the day of the picnic with the Bowers. For various reasons, Martyn wasn't particularly looking forward to it. She hadn't come out west to socialize, but to help a sick girl. However, there was no means of escape, for who, on a burningly hot day, could refuse to go on a picnic by the river? Who, that is, except Poppy, who seemed quite capable of avoiding all social commitments and appeared to have come to Diamond Springs to make curtains and to gossip with the cook. And, on the side, Martyn more than suspected, to upset her stepson's matrimonial plans, if she possibly could.

The picnic was not, as far as Martyn was concerned, a success. They didn't start off till afternoon, and while Fay monopolized Red – or should it have been the other way about? – David was intent on monopolizing Martyn, and weakly, she agreed to take a walk along the river bank with him when she would far sooner have been in the water with the others.

'What do you do with yourself at Diamond Springs all day, Martyn?' David asked as they strolled slowly along. 'Do you go out on the run with Red? Are you a horsewoman as well as a swimmer?'

She shrugged. 'I'm not a horsewoman, I can ride a bit – now. But I don't go out on the run.'

'I'm surprised at that.' He added casually, 'You do realize, don't you, that he and my sister are probably going to be married soon? It's something you should know, because I'm willing to bet old Red was at least part of your reason for coming outback.'

Martyn felt a strange constriction in her chest. She said briefly in an off-putting way, 'I'm years younger than Red. And than you too.'

His light amber-coloured eyes laughed at her. 'That's not so old – Red and I are about the same age, thirty-three.'

Martyn felt a little shock of surprise. Red was only thirty-three! She had thought him five or six years older than that. Perhaps it was his heavy build, his air of authority, of power. Subtly, it seemed to alter her focus on him . . .

David went on, 'You should have come to stay at Jindi-yindi instead of at Diamond Springs. I'd have seen to it you had a good time. The old homestead needs a bit of modernizing, but it's not uncomfortable. What about it? Any chance of making a move?'

'Not the slightest,' she said, sure he couldn't possibly be serious. 'I'm Poppy's guest.'

'Does Poppy drive you around? – entertain you?' he asked sceptically – as if he too knew about the other girls, and of Poppy's probably unsubtle tactics.

'Sometimes,' she lied. 'But I can entertain myself.'

'Doing what?' They had slowed to a stop under a giant gum tree, and he had turned to face her, and she was impressed anew by his good looks.

'Oh, I ride around, I swim. As a matter of fact, I caught up with some emus the other day. I'm going to look for them again soon to see if they usually come that way.'

'Where was this?' he asked idly, his eyes roving over her face and down the length of her figure.

Nervous under his rather rude regard, she told him in detail, and found herself chattering on, ill at ease, with a rather full description of the chicks. 'They're absolutely fascinating,' she finished.

He came a couple of steps closer. 'Not half as fascinating as you,' he said softly. He put his arms around her, locking his fingers behind her waist and swaying her towards him. 'Are you going to let me kiss you?'

She hadn't even got around to saying a very decided No when quite abruptly he let her go, for the simple reason that Red had come striding towards them, to saying imperiously and unsmilingly, 'If you two don't come and take a swim, it will be too late.'

Martyn snatched at the excuse to get away, but was furious that Red should have caught her with David's arms around her. Red-cheeked, she marched ahead of the others back towards the picnic. Fay had come out of the water and stood in her bikini in the sun. Ignoring her, Martyn went straight to the car and changed quickly into her green swimsuit. Back at the water, she dived in quickly and was completely disconcerted on surfacing, to find herself at very close quarters with Red, whom she had not even noticed in the water. She flipped back her wet hair and blinked some of the water from her lashes, confused at encountering the splintery sharpness of grey eyes.

'Disappointed it's not David?' he asked mockingly.

'Maybe,' she said, and added senselessly, almost as though to cover up something else, 'Why did you have to come and shove your frame in just now, anyhow?'

'I thought it might be prudent,' he said unsmilingly.

She gave him an angry baffled glance, then ducked her head down and swam underwater as far as she could until lack of breath forced her to surface. She looked back and he was threshing towards her – swimming fast but with appalling lack of style. He slowed when he saw her, and when he was close enough she saw his eyes were blazing angrily.

'You little idiot! Are you trying to drown yourself – to give everyone a fright?'

She stared at him in amazement. 'Neither. There's nothing to make a fuss about. There aren't any snags here and I've been swimming since before I could walk, I'm perfectly safe.'

He was white about the nostrils. 'I just don't like

pranks of that kind. You're never to do that again. Never. Do you understand?' He glared, then turned his back on her and swam back towards the bank. Without a second's thought, she followed him, and by putting on a spurt managed to pass him and scramble on to the bank ahead of him with a sense of angry triumph.

'That's not tactful,' David said in her ear after she had picked her way across the spiky grass and reached for her towel. 'No man likes a woman to beat him at any sport. You're certainly some swimmer, aren't you? Don't ask me to have a race – I'll be completely demoralized.' She looked at him, but she scarcely saw him, though she smiled coolly, and she was hardly aware of it when he put his hand on her bare back. 'Why do you wear that cover-up thing? Don't you have a bikini?'

'No. My sister-in-law didn't think it would be the best gear to wear in the bush where I might be swimming with the stockmen or – anybody.' As she spoke her eyes looked for Red and found him, further along the bank with Fay, half naked in her tiny two-piece. 'Bikinis are all right if you don't take swimming seriously. I find a one-piece the most comfortable.' She swung her gaze back to David.

'The most comfortable way to swim,' he said deliberately, 'is in the nude.'

She coloured slightly. 'Here? One couldn't.'

'Why not? On a lovely warm moonlight night—'

Red had moved a few steps closer. He asked coldly, 'What are you two talking about?'

David grinned. 'Swimming in the nude. Preferably by moonlight.'

Martyn felt she could have died, and Fay looked disgusted.

'For heaven's sake, David, remember Martyn's just a kid.'

Just a kid? Who had put that into Fay Bower's mind? Martyn needed just one guess. She said smilingly, 'What makes you think so, Fay? I'm sure if you ask Red about the things I got up to in Sydney he'll put you straight about *that*.'

She could see fury in Red's eyes and a very curious expression in Fay's. David said, alert, 'Oh, so you two knew each other that well in Sydney, did you?'

'No, we did not.' Red spoke almost savagely. 'Don't jump to the conclusion either that I was mixed up in any of Martyn's escapades. What's more, I won't have anyone swimming nude on Diamond Springs. And that I mean.' He turned away abruptly. 'Now I suggest we get a fire going. It's going to turn cool here by the water – hardly the evening for stripping off and jumping in, rather fortunately.'

No, it was not a successful picnic. Martyn was thankful when it was all over, the last chop eaten, the last bit of mess cleared away, everyone beginning to yawn, herself most of all.

On the way back to the homestead – thankfully a short drive – Red said into the darkness, 'You don't beat about the bush, do you, Martyn? A new romance under way already. Do *all* personable older men draw you like a magnet?'

'You mean David?' she asked resignedly.

'Who else? I don't know that I'd consider it the best way to help you sort out your personal problems. It may possibly wean you off the idea that the big romance of your life is connected with a man easily twice your age, but all the same—'

'All the same, if I want *your* advice, the thing would be to say a great big NO to David,' Martyn broke in swiftly. Too swiftly, because she didn't stop to think.

'There's an interesting reaction,' he said instantly. 'I can't imagine David's asked you to marry him already, so am I to conclude he's made you a different proposition? If that's the case, certainly my advice would be to say No. Further – it would be not to *invite* such propositions in future.'

There was silence for five seconds. Martyn seethed and regretted that her lack of experience made it impossible for her to find a smart and worldly retort. Her own fault of course for opening her mouth too wide too soon. It was something she'd have to watch as far as Red Diamond was concerned. Then he said musingly, 'I've seen my sisters through various love affairs, various aberrations, but I'll admit, I've never dealt with anyone quite as tricky and enigmatic as you, Martyn Verity. One of these days I'm going to find out whether or not you're somewhat ahead in emotions and experience of the wholesome schoolgirl type you assuredly typify – at least outwardly.'

'Are you really? And just how will you do that?'

'You'd be surprised,' he said dryly.

She couldn't see his face – only a dim shape and occasionally the glint in his eyes as he turned to face her. The headlights of the car leaped ahead on the track, made ghosts of the trees, intensified the dark of the outback. It was as if she and the man beside her were alone in the world. And yet, just minutes ahead, was the station homestead. Poppy, Mrs. Hall. The men's quarters, the small cottage where Elsey was minding Drummer's children while his wife was in hospital.

Out of her thoughts she asked, 'Has Drummer's wife had her baby?'

'Yes.' He sounded surprised.

'Is it a boy or a girl?'

'A boy.'

'I suppose he's pleased.'

'Why on earth do you suppose that?'

'Because he has two girls already. And *they* want a brother. What are they calling him?'

'Tancred,' he said, slight amusement in his voice, though under the amusement she sensed a sort of pride, a gentleness, that were strange in him. 'So you've been making friends among the aborigines. You're an odd girl.'

'Am I? I don't know how you work that out. What do you expect me to do all day? I have to entertain myself somehow.'

'I suppose you do,' he conceded. 'However, you *would* come.'

'Because I thought I was going to be useful,' she said quickly. He was driving so slowly the car seemed scarcely to be moving at all. 'It's true, even if some nasty suspicious streak in your nature won't let you believe it.'

'Okay, okay, we've been through all that before. But just don't hold me responsible for your predicament. If you stop still and think for just two seconds you might remember I warned you not to come to Diamond Springs.'

She gave an exasperated sigh. Because he was an exasperating man, and trying to get through to him was like trying to walk through a stone wall. She suggested, 'Mightn't it have been better if you'd told your stepmother not to invite me – or to cancel the invitation out? You're the boss here, aren't you?'

He disregarded that. He said, 'You're sorry you came?'

Was she sorry? Ahead, she could see the lights of the homestead. At least, there was just one light shining on the verandah. Around the men's quarters there was complete darkness. She heard a dog bark and then there was silence till from a long way off there came a drumming sound – the sound she had heard her first night in the outback. She thought briefly of his question and it was an unanswerable one, because for some strange reason she simply could not conceive of not having come to Diamond Springs – of not being here, alone in the car with Red Diamond, on this very night – engaging with him in an irritating, bewildering, unsatisfactory yet somehow – *fascinating* – conversation.

So instead of answering his question, she asked one of her own.

'What's that drumming sound?'

'It's an emu,' he said. 'Probably the female warning her mate of danger.'

It came again, just once, and then the silence of the bush closed in. Martyn said softly, 'I love to hear it. It's an exciting sound. I don't miss the sea so much when I hear sounds like that.'

'The bush is full of sounds,' he said. 'Can't you hear them?'

They had reached the precincts of the homestead now, and he switched off the engine and the headlights. The car windows were wide open and they sat and listened. It was so dark now that when she turned her head a little she could barely see his profile, against the only slightly lesser dark of the night. They were both silent, listening. Martyn heard a faint night wind in the trees, the soft sighing of the leaves as they moved infinitesimally. She heard a stealthy rustling on the ground nearby amongst the fallen gum leaves and strips of bark. She heard the soft hesitant call of an owl.

Yes, the night had its sounds, and she turned slightly to tell him and observed that his profile was no longer towards her. He had shifted a little, so silently and cautiously that she had not been aware of it. Now his arm was along the back of the seat behind her shoulders, and though it was not touching her, she could feel its warmth. Suddenly she was too aware of him beside her in the darkness of the car. Red Diamond – a man who sometimes infuriated her, a man who – she had to admit it – intruded too often on her thoughts. Ignore him she could not. He had some kind of fascination for her.

He spoke, and his voice was rough, edgy. '*I'm* sorry you came, Martyn Verity. You're going to be a problem to more than one person around here. It's a very great pity my stepmother asked you along.'

'I don't know what you're getting at,' said Martyn half indignantly. 'She asked me because of Jan and so that—' She stopped. She had never confided her problems to Red. And wasn't it best to let him think what he did?

His fingers tugged in a disturbing way at a lock of hair that fell almost to her shoulder. 'So that what?' he asked remorselessly. 'So that you could get away from Bastian Sinclair for a while? Though I'll guarantee you've never told *her* who your boy-friend is.' His fingers had released her hair, and now they touched the side of her neck, so delicately that she wasn't sure if she was imagining it or not. Because Red's fingers were simply not delicate. And besides, why would he touch the side of her neck like that? She felt herself grow tense, and though she held her head quite still, something went wild in her. Right now she couldn't get anything sorted out. She wondered why they were sitting here in the dark together – talking about what, she didn't know. Her mind was a mad, mixed-up kaleidoscope of picture and sensation, and she said incoherently, 'I – I don't want to talk about it – my – my problems.'

'No?' She felt his eyes reaching for her, through the darkness, and then he moved nearer and his fingers caught the lobe of her ear and pulled it gently. Yet it was the most excruciatingly tantalizing sensation she had ever experienced. She caught her breath. She wanted to cry out, and she wanted to lay her face, her cheek, against his hand and capture it against the soft bareness of her neck. And that was what she did.

After that, the inevitable happened. She was in his arms, and oh, they were powerful arms. And his mouth – it didn't seek hers, but it was on her eyelids, her temples – her throat. Gently, gently – hovering only. He needed a shave – not badly, but quite definitely – and while one part of her was quite lost, while her hands had gone of their own accord to lie flat, fingers spread, against his back, warm beneath the soft cotton of his shirt – another part of her was almost shocked, and completely bewildered. It had been strange enough to think she was here alone in the car with him, but for this to happen, out of the blue – to be in his arms—

And then she recollected. He was going to find out how she stood in regard to emotion and experience.

It was like a dash of icy water in her face. He was not going to find out. Not anything. Particularly what she didn't know herself. If his lips found hers, she might hate it. She might. But she was doubtful. She just didn't know how she would react – and she didn't want him to make the experiment, to find out—

She stiffened and withdrew.

'Enough?' he said softly – mockingly. She wished she could see his face and in some strange way she hated him because she couldn't. And she hated him for the way he asked her, so coolly and clinically, 'Enough?' She had the feeling she was trapped, that he *had* found out something and that whatever it was, it was not to Martyn Verity's advantage.

She didn't say another word to him before they parted for the night.

# CHAPTER SEVEN

AFTER the day of the picnic, Martyn was determined to make a really serious effort to avoid even a moment alone with Red. David had warned her that Fay and Red would probably be married soon, and it was embarrassing to think she had been thrown in his path deliberately by Poppy. The slightly humiliating part of it all was that she couldn't really feel herself to be in any way exclusive. Poppy, nice as she was, was an interfering matchmaker, and Martyn was just one more girl in the line – perhaps a last bid at a time when things, from Poppy's point of view, were getting rather desperate. Red had – what was the phrase Poppy used? – 'Loved and dropped' a number of girls, but Fay Bower looked like not qualifying for the dropped category. As for the 'loved', Martyn knew nothing about that.

'And everyone's in the know,' thought Martyn, riding moodily out across the paddock the following day. 'I'm a late nomination for the position of Mrs. Tancred Diamond.' It was a thought that made her singularly uneasy. Mrs Tancred Diamond. Imagine belonging here – so far from the sea. Impossible? She might have thought so once, but now she wasn't sure . . .

Earlier in the day Poppy had shown her a big map of the Diamond Springs run, a map that took in the outskirts of the neighbouring properties, including Jindiyindi, and while she had talked, her finger pointing out a dam here, holding yards there, a river crossing and so on, Martyn's mind had strayed off on journeys of its own. *That* was where she had seen the emus; and there, on the far side of the trees, was a waterhole. So, thought Martyn, the mother emu could have been taking her chicks there. And *that* was the track she had travelled with Red, and *that* was the camp where they had been branding the calves . . .

Now, though she rode across a seemingly endless paddock, she knew almost exactly where she was, and her thoughts went compulsively to the man she had determined to avoid. A man who was too tough and hard to be sentimental about love, who had never 'worn rose-coloured glasses', and to whom the challenge of Jindi-yindi meant much, she was certain, despite the fact he had told Poppy it was a side issue. It was curious how he had touched her last night in the car, his fingers so gentle, his lips so caressingly soft – but *deliberately* so, she reminded herself quickly.

Do things just happen? Or do they happen because you want them to? she wondered. Or *not* happen because you *don't* want them to. Poppy had said, the first time they met, that she didn't believe in accidents of a particular kind – meaning Red and Martyn meeting accidentally on the beach. Well, that *hadn't* been an accident because Martyn had chased him into the sea. So now – had she in fact chased him to the outback? Had there been something else there all the time, hidden under her outward dislike of Red Diamond?

Her thoughts broke off. Away ahead of her, on the far side of the fence, an emu was racing, and to her amazement she saw that one emu – maybe six feet tall, and with the tiniest head you could imagine, but what muscular legs! – kick the wire fence, break it, and go through. Martyn, who had reined in her horse, stopped and stared. In the next paddock there were sheep. She could see them dotted about amongst the hummocks of grass and under the shade of the belahs. They were sheep kept for killing, as a change from the perpetual beef. It was something she had learned that morning when Poppy showed her the map. The paddock where they were kept was small, and she watched the emu stalking across it in a lordly way, looking this way and that, while a few of the sheep looked up and then began to drift, as if drawn by an invisible current, towards the hole in the fence.

Broken fences, as everyone in the outback knew – even

115

Martyn – meant trouble. She stayed quite still, thinking. Sketched on her retina was that map of Diamond Springs. She knew where the men were working today, and that there was a gate in the fence some distance back. But she didn't need the gate, she could take her horse through the break in the fence and make her way to the paddock that was being mustered just a little bit more quickly.

It didn't take much longer than she had thought, and it wasn't hard to locate the working camp. There wasn't all that much dust, because there was still plenty of feed on the ground after the rains, but where there are a lot of cattle there is always a bit of dust.

She shaded her eyes and looked over at the men as she came nearer to the camp. She couldn't see Red, and that was just as well, seeing she wanted to avoid him. Mostly the men with the cattle appeared to be aboriginal stockmen – she couldn't even see that rangy character who was Red's overseer. But she caught sight of one man she recognized, amongst the bright checked shirts and broad-brimmed hats. The aboriginal Drummer, and she rode over and told him what had happened.

His big white teeth showed in a smile.

'Those emus! That two times they done that. I'll tell the boss, miss. He be here d'rectly.'

Martyn didn't move away at once, though the thought of Red being here 'd'rectly' made her feel guilty. He'd think she was chasing him up when she had determined to do quite the opposite . . . She asked Drummer, 'How is the new baby? You called him Tancred, didn't you?'

'Too right! He's fine – come home soon to Diamond Springs. Teach him grow up be a fine stockman, work for Red like me.' He paused, then added a word of warning. 'That paddock next the killing sheep – you watch out for emus in the long grass, miss.'

Martyn said she would and out of the tail of her eye she saw Red come riding up, and she turned in the saddle ready to hear, 'What the hell are you after, mermaid?'

Instead, he merely cocked his eyebrows and asked laconically, 'How did you find the camp, Martyn?'

She coloured a little and put her head up. Drummer had moved away a little, very discreetly. 'Poppy showed me on the map.'

'And Poppy thought you could make it out here without mishap?'

Her colour deepened. 'I had no intention of coming here,' she said aloofly. She knew *Poppy* had had it in mind. 'But I happened to see a break in one of your fences, and the killing sheep are coming through the gap. I thought I'd better let someone know.'

His eyes were watching her intently, and now he frowned. 'Those damned emus again, I suppose. Right – thanks for the news, you've been helpful. Can you find your way home again?'

'Yes, thank you. Good-bye,' she said abruptly, and wheeled her horse. She sent Dummer a wave, and was off, away from Red Diamond, forcing herself to forget him and to think of those emus that she had meant to look for and to draw.

She was back again the following day. Not at the muster camp, but looking for the emus and the chicks. And by late afternoon, with her wild-life drawings done, she'd sought out a place where she could stretch out and take a rest – a place where the ground was comparatively soft and red and sandy, in the shade of some feathery-leaved acacias. She was wearing a pair of old jeans she had brought and a pink cotton button-through blouse. Already the jeans were grubby from the time she had spent crawling about, hiding behind – or in! – tall clumps of uncomfortably spiky grass, so she could get closer to her prey.

She had seen two other adults as well as the one with the chicks, and at one stage one of them had actually stalked her while she was stalking its friend! In fact, it had sneaked up on her to investigate while she was busily drawing. It had approached her from the side, and peered down to look at her sketches and she had nearly jumped out of her skin. She had kept quite still, those weird eyes had blinked at her, one pearly plastic button was picked deftly from her blouse – taking a scrap of cotton material with it – and then, its curiosity satisfied, the emu had gone on its way unhurriedly.

After a moment of complete disbelief, Martyn had laughed aloud.

Now all the excitement was over, the emus had vanished into the scrub, Martyn lay on her stomach watching the shadows moving over the red earth and thinking out her story and its possibilities. A slight breeze had come up and the trees, where she had left her horse, made a hushing sound. It wasn't in the least like the hushing sound made by the sea, it was plainly and unmistakably an outback sound. A few birds flew about – no seagulls wheeling and screaming here! – but little bluebonnets, black and white magpies, a number of roguish galahs.

The bush. The outback.

Lying on the red sand – on the very bosom of the land – that received her warmly, securely, steadily. No lulling rocking motion, no glitter of sun or white coral sand. And when her tongue touched her lips and tasted salt, it was the salt of her own sweat. But oh! it was a fact that sea and salt and sand weren't everything in life, even if you had been born to them and had lived with them for the whole of your nineteen years. The red heart of this country called to her as strongly as did its golden shores, and it was all confused with the dark image of a man with eyes that burned with the fire of diamonds . . .

Martyn started out of a kind of dream as a shadow blotted out the sunlight that touched her through moving leaves. She blinked her blue eyes open, her heart pounding, and jerked herself into a sitting position. Against the dazzling blue of the sky, she saw a man on horseback. Red! Then her heart dived. It was David Bower.

He smiled down at her, then swung down from the saddle to the ground.

'Hello, beautiful. I was looking for you. I saw your horse back there in the trees, but it took me a few minutes to locate you. You're well camouflaged there in your dusty pink, and as still as a goanna sunning itself. What have you been dreaming about?'

As he spoke, he lowered himself to the ground beside her and putting an arm around her pulled her body lightly against his own. Martyn resisted because it was instinctive. She scrambled to her feet, and he got up too, to stand, hands on hips, looking at her quizzically.

'What's making you so edgy? You're perfectly safe with me.'

'I'm cramped,' she said. It seemed the easiest thing to say. She stretched her arms above her head and wished vainly that she hadn't stayed so long. She had meant to be back at the homestead by this, in time to shower and clean up for dinner. She glanced at David frustratedly. He looked very handsome, very civilized, in his cream shirt, smart riding breeches and boots. His horse, obviously a thoroughbred, stood quietly under the trees.

He said, 'I don't see nearly enough of you. You've been on my mind ever since the picnic – when Red came and broke it up just as I was about to kiss you. You didn't give me a chance after that, did you? Was it deliberate?' He stood close to her, half-smiling down into her face. Looking back, she thought his eyes were cold, devoid of expression as if a screen had been drawn across them.

She said indifferently, fidgeting a little, 'It just happened that way.'

'So why are you trying to avoid me now? On Sunday you were perfectly happy to have me kiss you—'

'You didn't kiss me,' she interrupted.

'But I was about to, and you knew it. Yet just now – the way you scrambled away from me – well, it wasn't flattering.'

Martyn sighed. 'I don't particularly like kissing people,' she said, flushing.

His eyes roved over her. 'That's something I've never

yet heard a pretty girl say – and mean.' He took a step closer and reached for her hands, but she put them quickly behind her back.

'*I* mean it,' she said.

'I thought you liked me.'

'That doesn't mean I want you to kiss me.' She glanced at her watch. 'Anyhow, it's time I was going home.'

'Home,' he repeated, frowning. 'To Red Diamond? Are you in love with him? Because if so, it's sheer waste. I've told you he and Fay are serious about each other. You're a rank outsider. It's common knowledge that Poppy brought you along because she doesn't like the Bowers, and that's just one more reason why you're not going to do any good for yourself. Red doesn't like to be pushed – and he doesn't like to be chased, either. Did you know that? He's a man who prefers to make his own decisions.'

Martyn's colour was high. It was unpleasant to be told she had designs on Red. She said levelly, 'I know that. And I'm perfectly satisfied to let him do so.' Her eyes challenged him. 'Are you?' Because she was pretty sure David was very interested in seeing Red and his sister team up, and Diamond Springs money flowing across the paddocks into Jindi-yindi.

Above, the sky was paling and the tree shadows were lengthening across the ground. Though she hadn't meant to say it, Martyn remarked, 'I just wonder why Fay and Red didn't marry long ago.'

'Meaning that my sister's older than you are? Well, my dear, not every man likes to take on the task of teaching love to an ex-schoolgirl. And I don't think you're much more than that yet, are you?'

'Not much,' she agreed levelly, but she felt wounded. It was true, and perhaps that was the whole trouble. She had reached the stage of wanting to be more than a raw little ex-schoolgirl, and for the first time she wished Bastian had taught her something about love. Yet she had recoiled from the one lesson he had tried to teach her. She was still – Red had put it into words – reading the first primer. Bastian had started too much in advance for her, but David – Her eyes narrowed and she looked at him speculatively. Here was a man who could teach her something, if not about love, at least about its arts. Kissing – So why refuse the lesson she so badly needed? How much had she to learn before she could even *start* to learn! That was the paradox.

David said lazily, 'Fay and Red are mature people – they understand each other. I suppose you know that Lewis Bower was in love with Fay – someone will have told you. As for Red, he hasn't lived the life of a monk. But he's ready to settle down now, and she's the obvious choice.'

'You mean they love one another?' It was a ridiculous conversation, and Martyn rather thought that later she was going to wish she could forget it. She was aware that David was underlining very heavily the fact that she didn't have a chance with Red, and though when she first came outback it would all have bounced off her, somewhere along the line everything had changed.

David said, 'I would presume so.' He smiled down into her eyes, and when he reached for her hands this time, she let him take them and draw her towards him. He said softly, 'You're young, but not too young for me. You're adorable.' And then his arms were around her and his lips touched hers.

It was a flavourless, meaningless kiss. If Martyn had hoped to learn a lesson in love, then she was badly disappointed. His mouth against hers, his arms embracing her – deliberate, calculated – it was *nothing*.

She didn't know till David released her, and with one arm still lightly around her waist turned slightly, that a station wagon had driven up. Now she both saw it and heard it break to a stop, the door flew open, and Red Diamond got out and stalked towards them, the red light of sundown on his face.

It was the first time she had seen him as red instead of

black, and her eyes widened as he covered the few paces between them. His wild black hair, his strong, dark-browed face, his muscled forearms emerging from the rolled up sleeves of a black shirt – all were burnished by the rich red light lavished on them from a sky that had turned into a blaze of crimson and vermilion fire. She caught the flash of his eyes. Red Diamond. How well the name suited him! Something in Martyn's breast leaped up like a living flame to meet him, to salute him. She was totally unaware of the other man who stood so close to her, one arm possessively around her waist. One image only filled her mind. Hard as diamonds? She supposed so. She had certainly never seen a soft side to his nature. And yet—

His voice broke almost brutally into her dizzying thoughts.

'You'd better come along home with me, Martyn, now I've located you – and put Poppy's mind at rest. In her psychic way, she was quite convinced that something drastic had happened to you when you didn't turn up at your accustomed hour,' he added dryly. He gestured back to the car. 'I brought Drummer along to track you ... I thought you were going to the cattle sales, David.'

'I changed my plans,' said David shortly. 'Fay and I talked it over and decided those stores were not for us – we're more interested in buying good breeding stock.'

The diamond eyes didn't flicker and there was no expression on Red's face as he said briefly, 'I see.'

'I'd meant to come and talk it over with you, but—' David shrugged and stopped, and Martyn could practically hear Red's unspoken question— 'But what?'

Instead, he said somewhat curtly, 'You must run things your way. Jindi-yindi's your show, not mine, and you're' – his grey eyes looked hard at the other man – 'you're an experienced countryman. Come along now, Martyn.'

Of course she went, but first she looked up into David's face to say, 'Good-bye. Be seeing you.' And then at the car, from which Drummer had emerged to take over her horse, she looked back at David to remark, 'That's a beautiful horse of David's. And doesn't he ride it beautifully?'

Red said nothing for a moment. Then— 'That horse cost a packet. The man might do better to breed horses instead of trying to resuscitate a hungry, half dead cattle station.'

Somehow Martyn knew he disagreed completely with the course David was following in regard to buying stock. For her part, she didn't know a thing about station affairs, but she agreed wholeheartedly with Red's pronouncement that David must run things his own way. Of course, when Red married Fay, then he'd have a finger in the pie – and wouldn't he give it a stirring up! She thought, 'There'll be arguments – and I can guess who'll win.' David would be driven away. Was that what Red wanted?

She got into the car beside Red. Her protest that she could ride home was ignored. Drummer was obeying orders.

'I want to talk to you, Martyn,' Red said uncompromisingly.

She didn't ask about what. Just because David had kissed her, she supposed she was in for a lecture, though what business it was of Red's she couldn't imagine. And was soon to discover.

He wrenched the car into gear, swung it around, and they charged across the paddock.

'How often does this happen?' he fired at her.

Martyn blinked. 'It's hardly your business,' she retorted. 'I don't have to tell you how often another man kisses me—'

He uttered an impatient exclamation. 'Forget the kissing game. That doesn't interest me. All I want to know is how often you spend the afternoon with David Bower.'

'That's my business, too.'

'Not entirely,' he snapped back. He turned his head sharply, his glance going to the open neck of her blouse. She raised her hand defensively, and discovered the missing button – the button the emu had nipped off. 'You're a guest at Diamond Springs, and I'm not going to turn an entirely blind eye if you come back to the homestead with half the buttons missing from your clothes. However, at present all I'm interested in is how much time my neighbour has been wasting on you – time that would be better spent in an effort to straighten out a property that's badly in need of intelligent handling. I want to know if the delights of your company are so strong as to make him forget a mere cattle sale. Or if the real reason he forgot was because he'd spent too much cash on thoroughbred horses . . . Had you made a date with him for today?'

'No,' said Martyn, her cheeks pink. She felt taken down a peg or two quite decidedly. Her self-interest must make her look very small in his eyes. 'This is the first time David and I have met on your property – except last Sunday – so I hope he may be absolved from that particular parcel of guilt. Your honour,' she added ironically.

He gave her a sharp look but no answer at all. When she glanced at him he was frowning, and thinking no doubt of David's sins and omissions rather than of hers. But when he spoke again, it was to ask, 'What do you do with yourself all day? Poppy says you disappear most afternoons – go out riding. You'll get lost one of these days.'

'No, I shan't. I have a good sense of direction. Anyhow, I like coming out this way.'

'What's out this way?' he asked suspiciously.

'Emus,' said Martyn, and was answered by a short laugh of sheer disbelief that *that* could be her interest.

That night after Poppy had gone to bed, and while Red was still in the office, Martyn worked rather frenziedly on her drawings at the verandah table near her bedroom. The whole events of the afternoon had unsettled her in some way, and she didn't want to think about them. She tried hard to become totally absorbed in her drawings of the emu and its chicks, and the two small children who were to become involved with them, but it seemed almost impossible to stop herself from thinking about Red and Fay.

It was late when something made her look up, and there almost beside her was the man who had been in her thoughts. He had actually set a tray of drinks down at the end of the table and she hadn't been aware of it. Now he was watching her intently, and she wondered if, from his look of slight amusement, she had been drawing with the tip of her tongue out, a mannerism that had amused Bastian many times. She looked back at him almost guiltily, and the colour flooded her cheeks as she pushed back the fair hair that had fallen across her cheek.

'You're an unknown quantity, aren't you?' he commented. He reached for her sketch pad and began to turn the pages carefully. 'These are natty – and they're clever too. Except,' he added with a crooked smile, his grey eyes searching hers, 'you've got the wrong idea who brings up the chicks in the emu family. That's father emu's task. And in fact it's the male that incubates the eggs. He then looks after the young for about two years while mother emu, except for playing sentry, generally has a good time.' He put down the sketch book. 'Are you going to have a gin and lemon with me, or don't you drink with the enemy?'

How seriously did he mean *that*? Not too seriously, she decided, as she gave him a wry smile and said, 'I will have a drink, thank you.'

'I didn't know you were an artist as well as a swimmer,' he said a moment later as they sipped their long cold drinks.

'I'm not really,' she said diffidently. 'Drawing was about the only thing I was good at at school, but I wasn't clever enough to get a scholarship. Stan would have sent me to private classes, but that would have meant going to Sydney and I was happy living up the coast with him.'

He nodded, serious now. 'You were very close to your father?'

'Yes. I was the baby of the family, you see – well, there were only two of us, and my brother is twelve years older than I am. My mother died when I was small, then Dick went away to university and there were just Stan and me left. He was manager of the swmming baths.' As she spoke, she was remembering what he had said about her a few days ago – that she was spoiled, and so on, and hadn't had to earn her own living. She had an idea he was surprised to hear what her father's job had been, and somehow she was glad she had told him. He didn't speak, and she went on rather hurriedly, 'Stan always wanted me to have drawing lessons. He had a – a positively inflated opinion of my gifts. He was very – proud of me.'

'It's not surprising. You appear to have a lot of talent.' He reached for her glass and filled it up again. 'You're not going to tell me you're entirely self-taught, are you? These drawings' – tapping her sketch pad with a firm finger – 'appear to be practically professional standard.'

She flushed with surprise and pleasure at his praise. 'Thank you. I had some lessons from an elderly lady who'd retired up the coast, and then when I came to Sydney to live with Dick and Ros–' She hesitated, but he was waiting, so she went on, 'Bastian gave me lessons. Free,' she added, despite the hardening of his expression.

'Bastian Sinclair. Free private lessons. At his house.' He said it almost explosively, and looked at her accusingly.

'Why not?' she said defiantly. 'So you see, he's not just – not just an older man.' She raised her glass and drank the contents down quickly, knowing that her cheeks were hectic. The gin had something to do with it, but there were other causes as well.

'I see,' Red said, looking at her darkly. He had turned the reading lamp away so that there was only the glow of it reflected back from the off-white wall. 'And this – proposal of his – you're deciding whether it's worth taking a calculated risk and teaming up with a man who is art professor as well as a worshipper at the shrine of Aphrodite. I'd say it would be a highly unsuitable match, but you already know my opinion.'

He waited, and she didn't know what to say. Having Bastian there in the background was like having a lifebelt, in some way. If she admitted that she had broken with Bastian, that he had never proposed marriage to her, that her problem was something quite other – then she would be on her own. And floundering in waters too rough even for her to battle it out. She would be – swamped. She said uneasily, 'No matter what you think about Bastian, he's been – good to me.'

His lip curled cynically. 'Good to you? Yet your brother stopped the – drawing lessons, didn't he? And I suppose lecturing you makes you more pigheaded than ever. It's the old thing about forbidden fruit tasting the sweetest. And, as no doubt you're going to point out, *I* have no right to interfere in your diet. I wonder,' he concluded speculatively, 'how much – forbidden fruit you've already swallowed down? And if you've acquired a certain taste for it? Even what David Bower will hand out while you're in the throes of sorting out your priorities. No doubt Bastian Sinclair taught you a lot more than drawing in his house on the plateau. You wouldn't have been his first pupil, either. But of course that doesn't matter to you, does it?' He got to his feet slowly and deliberately, and reaching out took her empty glass and set it on the table. Then his fingers were clamped around her wrists and he pulled her to her feet. 'Here's something else for you to digest.'

She felt herself pulled against the hardness of his chest, and fear rose in her – fear that he would kiss her as Bastian had, because she was aware of something frighteningly fierce and primitive in his eyes – something too male and savage for her to contend with. If he only knew how limited was her experience in love – that David's kiss had been negative, that Bastian had kissed her only once and shocked the life out of her – that had been the full extent of *his* extra-curricular instruction – she heard herself gasp and twisted her head to one side to avoid the advance of his face towards hers.

Then she was crushed against the warmth of his body, and held so close she could feel and hear the heavy thumping of his heart. He held her hard so that she was completely helpless, and then one arm moved away while he switched off the reading lamp. Now, until her eyes readjusted, they seemed to be standing together in total darkness. His arm had come back to enfold her. Petrified, she thought – One kiss and another, and then you're eased all the way from the patio to the bedroom. *Her* bedroom door was just a few feet away, and there in the hot darkness her bed was waiting, the cover removed, the sheet turned down. If he wanted he could carry her there and all she would be able to do would be to yell. 'If you want something, let out a yell, and somebody will hear you . . .'

He spoke against her hair. 'What's the matter? Your heart's beating like you were some trapped creature – as if you were a bird that's been swooped on by a hawk.' One hand came to rest against her ribs by her heart, and her heart beat faster than ever as the warmth of his hand came through her thin cotton blouse with the heat of fire. Now her eyes were accustomed to the dark, she could see the shadowy shape of his face with its black brows, the wild black hair, the curve of the long mouth with its full and sensual lower lip. She could see the diamond glint of his eyes.

'Who does your heart beat for?' He dropped his face to hers, speaking once more against the silken fall of her hair. 'For your drawing teacher? For the handsome horseman from Jindi-yindi? Or is it expectation because I'm holding you like this – as if I were going to make love to you?'

'Don't dare,' she said huskily. 'I'll – I'll scream, I'll kick—' She paused to draw a much needed breath. 'Let me go! I – hate you, Red Diamond—'

'Hatred's a very convenient cloak to wear,' he mocked, his hold on her loosening not one fraction. 'Haven't you heard it said also that it's close to love? *Love* meaning whatever you choose it to mean ... I'm sure a girl who's already played around with a man of the world won't resist long once her senses have been roused by a few tricks.'

Martyn bit hard on her lip. His hand still rested where it could feel her heart and she breathed out, 'I just pity the girl you marry – you have no feeling – tricks are all she'll get, and tricks I despise—'

'Oh, come on now – David must have used a few tricks today, and you looked happy enough in his arms. If I hadn't come along, who knows what would have happened next? If you invite something, you usually get it. Haven't you learned that by now?'

'I – I didn't invite anything from you,' she bit out, though she was quaking. She had been right – he was too tough for her, far too tough. 'Do you want me to scream? Do you want – Poppy to come?'

He gave a low laugh, a diabolical sound that matched the darkness of his dimly seen face.

'Poppy? To see us here like this would delight my stepmother.' His lips moved to her temple and he added softly, 'Doesn't it delight you to be in my arms, Martyn Verity? Doesn't it?'

Martyn felt herself slump against him, as if she were about to faint. He was holding her suffocatingly close, and her arms, even with their strong swimmer's muscles, couldn't withstand him. In despair, she heard herself say on a moan, 'Do what you like—' Just what she meant by that she didn't know, whether it was surrender or pure defeat. But she thought wildly that if he took her at her word, there would come a moment when she would have the strength she needed to escape him. Because no one – not even Red Diamond – could do what they liked with Martyn Verity. It had never been that way. It never would ...

Quite suddenly she was released.

He reached out and switched on the lamp and swung it round so that it shone full and harsh on the two of them. Her face was bloodless, her eyes enormous, their pupils dilated. And she was shaking. He said harshly, 'Go to bed. The tricks *you* know just aren't in the book. I'm not going to carry you off by force. I simply imagined I was going to teach you a lesson.'

Martyn said nothing. She knew no tricks. *He* was the one who knew the tricks. He and David and Bastian. All of them older men, the older men whom he had accused her of – experimenting with, how long ago? But there was something in the way he played that baffled her. The axiom that Stan had taught her – Respect your body and others will do the same – didn't seem to have the same importance when he was around . . .

She turned away and moved blindly to her room. It was as he had told her back in Sydney. He could twist her round his little finger if he wanted to, and tonight, in fact, he had done exactly that.

And then, when he had done it, he had let her go. Underlining the fact he wasn't interested in waterbabies.

# CHAPTER EIGHT

AFTER that, it was as if there were a glass wall between herself and Red. She saw very little of him in the next few days, and even to encounter him briefly around the homestead, away from the dining-room table, was a kind of excruciating agony, they had so little to say to each other. In the mornings, he was gone long before she arose, and Poppy's frequent suggestions that he should take her out on the run were always pointedly ignored.

She no longer went to look for the emus, preferring not to risk encountering David there again, but she still went riding, or swam in the river, and the days went by quickly enough.

Jan Diamond was in the process of deciding on her wedding date. There had been a telephone call from Terrigal, but Poppy had not yet arranged with Red the exact day on which she and Martyn would leave Diamond Springs. Martyn knew that for her it would be all too soon. Her outback adventure was rushing to its end with frightening speed, and soon it would seem no more than a fleeting dream. One very real thing had happened, however. For the first time in her life she had fallen in love, and she couldn't see herself getting anything more than a broken heart. 'The hearts of the young are very pliant,' Red had said. Well, it was easy to talk when you were thirty-three ... There were times when Martyn wished she had never come but had accepted without protesting what fate most certainly had in store for her eventually — a course in typing.

When Poppy asked her that day over lunch on the verandah if she had 'nutted out' what she would do when she went home, she had to admit she was without inspiration. They had not talked together a great deal. Poppy was always busy, and now that the curtain-making was over, she had organized the girls into doing some very thorough house cleaning, which had begun the day before and was continuing on today. Red had said impatiently after dinner last night – before he did his customary disappearing act into the office – 'For God's sake, can't you leave it all to Mrs. Hall?'

'It's not her work,' said Poppy definitely. 'She has enough on her hands feeding the men and seeing the sweeping and dusting are done. The cupboards here are full of junk that hasn't seen the light of day for ten years or more. Your wife – when you take one – won't want to move in with all that.' She added almost accusingly, 'And by the way, Tancred, I'm putting a few things aside, some of them family things from way back – history, you might say. I'd like to take one or two bits of silver or china for the girls, so long as you don't think it's anything Fay will fancy particularly.'

Red frowned darkly at her. 'Take anything you want,' he said irritably. 'And just don't jump ahead of me. I haven't announced that I'm marrying Fay yet, have I?'

Listening, Martyn had wondered exactly what that meant. Simply that he hadn't *announced* it? Or did he mean he hadn't made up his mind? Well, either way, it could hardly affect Martyn Verity . . .

Now, as they sat over lunch, Poppy commented unexpectedly, 'Red says there's a man in your life, Martyn. Is it really serious?'

Martyn coloured deeply at her unexpected remark. There *was* a man in her life, and for Martyn it was serious. But it wasn't the man to whom Red had referred. She wondered if he had given Poppy any details and rather thought not. It had most likely been a stratagem to persuade his stepmother that it was no use trying to match Martyn up with him.

She said, deliberately evasive, 'Oh, my art teacher. I don't want to get married for ages yet.' She hurried on, 'I suppose the best thing after all will be to take that secretarial course when I go back.' As she said it, it seemed completely unreal. To go back to Ros and Dick and their bungalow – it was impossible to believe that in a very short time she would be whisked back into that other world and into an activity that had no appeal for her whatsoever. Even the thought of her beloved sea didn't comfort her. As for her picture-story book, it would probably never even get off the ground. All she would have would be some drawings that were a souvenir of her short stay on Diamond Springs.

'Well, it's your life,' said Poppy on a sigh. 'I had a silly idea I could help you some way – but I haven't. Still, we mustn't lose touch with you, Martyn. And you must certainly come to Jan's wedding. Tancred will come down for that. And I suppose Fay,' she added with a grimace.

Martyn said, 'Thank you,' and managed a smile, but she knew she wouldn't go to the wedding. She would disappear completely from Red's life, and he wouldn't even be aware of it.

Meanwhile, he was not going to have another chance to play havoc with her feelings. It wasn't as if she didn't know his opinion of her, and while hers of him had changed, and changed drastically, to him she was still, doubtless, a woolly-minded kid with a kinky taste for older men. 'But I don't have one for kids,' he had said, and the words were engraved indelibly on her mind. So too was the memory of those extraordinary moments with him when he had held her in his arms and hadn't kissed her. Once she had dreaded the possibility of his kiss, now she longed for it and knew it would never happen.

That afternoon she went down to the men's quarters to look for Drummer's children, meaning to sketch them – and so provide herself with another souvenir to cry over. It was hot and still, the leaves of the tall gum trees and the feathery pepper trees hanging straight and motionless. The little dog Noosa, playing in the dust with a half-rotten orange, growling at it, chasing it as if it were a ball, came racing up to greet her with a feverish wagging of its tail.

But there were no children to be seen, and presently a fat old aboriginal woman with a pipe between her teeth appeared and told her, 'That Elsey go walkabout – takem piccaninnies with um.'

Disappointed, Martyn thanked her and wandered back towards the homestead, but on the way decided she might as well go for a ride. That would be more profitable than dawdling around in the heat, and it no longer seemed important whether she should encounter David or not.

Soon she was riding away from the homestead into the peculiar silence and emptiness of the outback – over the unending plain that was patterned here and there by an island of trees around a waterhole, or the backwater of a river, its solitude and stillness rippled now and again by shadows as a flock of corellas flew across the face of the sun; by parrots that showed brilliant colour against a grey-green background, by the dark shapes of slowly moving cattle.

Reaching trees that sheltered the greenish water of a billabong, she dismounted and wandered along the shore, watching the scarlet and blue dragonflies that hovered silently over the water's surface. Beyond, through taller trees, she came to the river that flowed unaccustomedly deep and slightly muddy between its banks, and suddenly she stopped and shaded her eyes and stared. A short way up, on the far side of the river, were two very small black children, clad in bedraggled cotton dresses. Staggering, they were dragging a great sheet of bark across the flat stones that lined the low bank of the river. This side, where Martyn stood, the bank was steep and made of red earth, but where the children were moving it was a kind of pebbly beach. Suddenly their bark raft was launched and by some miracle they both managed to clamber on to it, the older child almost going under when she missed her footing as she attempted to haul herself aboard.

Now they were both lying on their stomachs and the raft left the bank and began to move fast. It twirled around a few times and then began to float downstream.

It all happened very quickly, and even while she was watching, Martyn was stripping off her jeans and cotton shirt. Then she had kicked off her sandals and, slithering down the steep bank, launched herself into the water that flowed even faster than she had thought. Those were Drummer's children, and heaven knew what they were up to, but they were pretty soon going to be in trouble, that was for sure.

She struck out from the bank and swam towards the bark raft, which was spinning crazily downstream. The children were plainly bewildered and beginning to be frightened. The older one was making vain efforts to paddle with one hand, but this did little more than to upset the equilibrium of the raft. And now the smaller child had stopped lying on her stomach and was trying to stand up. As she swam, Martyn kept her eye on them, well aware that any moment now those children were going to tip themselves right into the river. Even if they could swim – and she was inclined to doubt that they could – they were very small and they would be at the mercy of the current. Martyn could only hope that she would be able to deal with the two of them somehow or other when it all happened.

She swam powerfully, and the whole incident took only seconds. She reached the raft in the nick of time – just as it was about to capsize – and managed to steady it. Two pairs of liquid brown eyes gazed at her helplessly, and she said loudly and firmly, 'Lie down flat, both of you – and keep still. I'm going to get you over to the bank.'

The low bank – where they had come from – would be her best bet, she realized, as gripping the edge of the raft firmly between her two hands she began to propel herself backwards to the shore, using strong leg movements and pulling the raft and children with her. A glance behind showed the shore was further away than she had hoped, and revealed also the fact that the pebble beach had ended, though the bank was sloping and much more negotiable than on the other side.

The children were babbling to her now, she caught the words Noosa, and Elsey and walkabout, and she concluded they had tired of the camp life and hungered for their puppy and the comforts of life near the homestead. So they had run away. And very likely would have been drowned if she hadn't happened along – though she hadn't completed her rescue yet, by any means. She didn't speak but saved her breath for the strenuous job of pulling the raft diagonally across the current, hoping desperately that she wouldn't strike any snags. The heavy rains that had fallen weeks ago and caused all the damage to Jindi-yindi had flooded this river too, for she could see debris stranded high up on the banks.

Suddenly the children became excited, and Martyn, who was beginning to feel the strain, yelled at them to keep still or they would drown themselves. She discovered the cause of their excitement seconds later when two large brown hands reached for the raft and a voice said commandingly, 'Let go, Martyn. I'll see this through. Get yourself to safety – downstream at least twenty feet or you'll be in trouble with that old dead tree.'

It was Red, of course, and with a slight gasp of relief she turned to face him. Across his broad shoulders that gleamed naked and brown in the harsh sunlight, she saw a tangle of grey branches knifing wickedly from the bank. He had taken over the raft and was swimming the way she had done now, but instead of obeying him, she swam round opposite him so that she could help by pushing or steadying, whatever was necessary. After all, two very precious little lives were involved! Across the primitive raft, she could see his dark head, his wet black hair, and the silvery flash of his grey eyes. It seemed to Martyn that she stared half hypnotized into those eyes for a long time.

Red knew his river well, for he steered the float to a small inlet in the river bank – clear of snags, away from the current, low enough to negotiate. And it was not until that moment, as they reached safety, that she remem-

bered she was wearing nothing but a minute pair of light
beige panties and a tiny matching bra. She waited, tread-
ing water, while Red picked up each child and dumped
her on the bank, and then his eyes found her and his dark
brows ascended.

'You next? Are you too done in to get out by yourself?'

She shook her head. She had sworn to herself there
would be no more private encounters with him, and
though now at least the children were with them, her
heart was beating hard. His face across the dinner table
when he was preoccupied with station affairs – or with his
plans for teaming up with the Jindi-yindi people, for all
she knew – was quite different from the face she saw now,
darkly tanned, the sunlit water reflecting up into his eyes
so that they were more than ever like diamonds. On the
bank the children waited docilely, none the worse for
their escapade, but obviously a little in awe of the boss
and expecting at least a scolding. They looked pathetic
bedraggled little mites, and Martyn hoped he would not
be hard on them. But she couldn't wait here to see what
happened. Her clothes were on the other side of the river,
how far upstream she didn't like to think.

Her teeth chattering a little from nerves, she told Red
offhandedly, 'I'll swim back to where I got in. My horse is
there.'

His eyes mocked her. 'You might rate yourself high as a
swimmer, but you're not going to make it up there against
the current, mermaid. In fact, I'm just not going to let
you try. There's been more rain up north and there could
be a few snags drifting down. It's not as safe as the sea,
you know.'

'Oh, it's all right, I'll manage,' she told him determinedly. She looked up at the children whose wet cotton
dresses were rapidly drying in the heat of the sun. 'You –
you look after the children. Forget about me.'

'You'll do as I say,' he said sharply, commandingly. His
eyes moved from her face to her bare shoulders showing

above the surface of the water. He certainly couldn't see through this rather muddy-looking water, but she bit her lip vexedly. It would suit her a lot better to battle across the river somehow, but she had the very distinct feeling she was going to have to do as he said.

He said unexpectedly, 'I presume you have *some* clothes on, Martyn,' and added half humorously, 'I did forbid nude bathing on Diamond Springs, didn't I? Well, it's no time to be prudish, whatever your state of undress. Come along now, or I shall have to take matters into my own hands.'

He moved towards her purposefully and she set her teeth. It was all very well not being prudish, but her panties and bra hadn't been designed for the beach and they were infinitely more revealing than a bikini. And besides, when you'd had four inches cut off your hair just recently, you couldn't really look forward to riding a horse like a shorn Lady Godiva for heaven knew how many miles across paddocks that, even if they should by a lucky chance be empty of stockmen, were still peopled by Red Diamond. Nor, near naked, her thoughts continued fantastically, could you expect to enjoy a walk, shoeless, through the bush.

He moved again, and, crazily, she ducked under the water. When she surfaced, to her relief he had hauled himself out of the water, and her embarrassed eyes discovered that he was wearing a pair of dark blue fitting briefs that could easily have been swimming trunks.

'I'll take pity on you, waterbaby,' he said with weary cynicism. 'I'll see these kids back to their camp in the mulga, and then I'll be back for you. I'll wear the trousers and you can have the shirt. But you're to get out of the water the minute my back is turned. Understand? You're not to attempt to swim back up the river. Do I have your promise? If not—' His eyes and the grim line of his mouth threatened her.

'I – I promise,' she quavered, almost ingratiatingly.

She watched him move off, a tall broad-shouldered

man with two tiny aboriginal children trotting at his heels. And then she drew a deep breath and climbed out on to the bank.

She stood in the sun and her sparse clothing dried in a matter of minutes, though her hair was still partly wet, and she felt – and looked, she was certain – as naked as could be. If only her things had been black or red or green – any colour but pale beige! Skin colour, in other words, lighter than the colour of her skin, actually ...

It was a ridiculous situation to be in, and there was nothing to do but grin and bear it. Even if she broke her promise, and then somehow got across to the other side of the river – even then she'd have problems, because she'd be a long way from her clothes and her horse. No, she definitely needed help. It was just unfortunate that it should have to be his ...

When he came back she had lapsed into a daydream, with the heat of the sun on her body and the glare from the water in her eyes, so that she started guiltily when he spoke, his voice remote and cold.

'Good God! For a moment I thought you were stark naked. Here, put this shirt around you and we'll see what we can do about taking you back to your own garments.' He stood five feet off, broad and brown and intimidating-looking with his gleaming torso, his black hair, and the narrow-legged trousers and boots he now wore. He tossed a navy shirt across to her and, colouring furiously, she caught it. She fumbled with the sleeves, managed to get into it and to fasten the buttons quickly, aware that he stood, arms folded, eyes narrowed, watching her. It reminded her of the time she had seen him at the Fleets' swimming pool, and somehow been made conscious for the first time of her nakedness.

Like Eve in the Garden of Eden, she thought irrelevantly, slanting a look across at him through lashes that were glistening gold in the sun. There was a tilted cynical smile on that sensual mouth of his, and he commented, to her discomfiture, 'Now, believe me, you look more seductive than ever . . . Come along. You'll be relieved to know that I've got a vehicle.'

Head bowed a little and too much aware of his physical nearness, she moved towards him, picking her way carefully through coarse grass and fallen strips of bark. Had she ever thought that he was not handsome? she wondered dazedly. He was utterly, devastatingly so. He made every other male in the world look insignificant, pallid . . .

He waited for her, and she edged past him nervily and jumped when he laid a hand on her shoulder.

'You're a funny little animal,' he said conversationally, not removing his hand despite the fact that he must be aware of her reaction. 'All self-confidence in the water, but on land as jumpy and nervous as a wildcat . . . Are you going to make it to the car barefoot? I drove as close as I could. Or shall I give you a lift?'

'I'll – I'll make it,' said Martyn. And at that moment, unnerved by his touch and moving too quickly, she stepped on a bindi-eye burr and let out an automatic cry of pain. In a flash he had scooped her up into his arms, and though she wasn't a small girl, he carried her as easily as if she had been a child, one arm beneath her bare thighs, the other around her shoulders. She didn't struggle, it would have been undignified, but she felt her own heart thudding and his too, and she felt distinctly naked, under the ridiculously large shirt.

'You've a fine pair of legs,' he said with cool admiration when he finally set her down near the car – an old and dusty-looking utility that was obviously general station property. She stood nervously in the red dust, longing to make some perky retort but quite simply unable to do so. Another few seconds and they were both in the car, but instead of starting up he turned and gave her a long thoughtful glance.

'Do you know you were acting quite in the old tradition, transporting those kids across the river on a bark raft? That's the way the aboriginals have been doing it from time immemorial.' His eyes, anthracite grey and keen, held something more in their depths than mere inquiry. They were just not quite impersonal, and they were definitely disconcerting. How can eyes do this to anyone? Martyn wondered, as she looked back into them compulsively, simply unable to look anywhere else – fascinated, swooning a little in the strange and almost fearsome delight of answering eyes like those. Eyes that belonged to a man she had begun by hating and now – and now hungered for.

Dazedly, she said, 'I didn't know. *They* found the piece of bark – I saw them launch it and I thought they might drown themselves. So—'

'So you didn't have a moment's hesitation in divesting yourself of your respectable clothing and going to the rescue. It was as well you did. I'd probably have arrived too late. I drove over to the camp to check up on their well-being – Drummer was a bit worried, Elsey's not all that reliable, and he hadn't wanted her to take them away. The blacks are camped in the mulga, the kids had grown homesick for their pup – and the good food.'

'I guessed as much.' She gave the ghost of a smile.

'You did? You take quite an interest in the domestic side of station affairs, don't you? Well, they're back with Elsey now, but someone will pick them up this evening and bring them back to the homestead. Mrs. Hall can take them in tow. Or Poppy. It might give her something a bit more useful to do than cleaning out cupboards.' His eyes raked over her once more, and then he added, 'I think you've taken to the outback. You get yourself around a bit, don't you?'

Yes, she got herself around. But she never went out to the muster where she wouldn't be welcomed. She said, 'It's not bad. But I prefer the sea.'

'Ah yes – the sea and all its associations. Well, are you ready to go back now?'

The question disconcerted her. Of course she was

ready. It wasn't her idea they should sit here all day exchanging glances and chit-chat ... Or did he mean – was she ready to go back to the coast? She raised her eyes and felt herself quail. He saw too much – his eyes looked too hard.

He said, 'Why are you so scared of me, mermaid?'

'I'm not,' she retorted. But she was – for reasons she could never tell him. She added, 'I just think you're hard – invulnerable—'

His eyes narrowed. 'Invulnerable? Well, it wouldn't be good for a man in my world to be too much the other way, would it? And hard – well, we've agreed before, I'm hard as diamonds. The old cliché. Though lately I've begun to question that.'

A long moment passed and she thought he was going to reach for her, she saw the muscles of his hard brown arms move, because he was naked from the waist up. Then instead he turned away from her and started up the motor. And she was – yes, she was disappointed, she, Martyn Verity! The shame of it! What had happened to her resolve – to her principles?

He drove rapidly along the river bank and finally they reached a rough-looking bridge and rattled their way across it cautiously. He said, 'We don't generally need this, only when the river's up,' and she nodded. Now they were heading back in the other direction to where she had left her horse, her clothes, and neither of them spoke again.

Her horse was there, and she located her clothes with only a little difficulty and got back into them, then rejoined him. He had left the car and stood, hands on hips, looking out over the paddocks, and now turned to face her, glancing over her as she stood there, respectable again in her old jeans and the green top. She handed back his shirt and as he got back into it, he drawled out, 'What's happened to the honeymoon gear you brought along, I wonder?'

'I keep that for the homestead,' she said pertly, though

she had coloured. 'There's no one to impress, riding around.'

'No? Well, you've impressed me today. Still, don't bother too much tonight. Any old thing will do.' He sent her an enigmatic smile and helped her up into the saddle. Then with a brief salute, he got back into the old utility and they had parted company.

On Saturday night the Bowers turned up at Diamond Springs; Martyn had no idea whether it was by invitation or not. Dinner was over and Poppy, Red and Martyn were, for once, all sitting together on the verandah.

Red got lazily to his feet the moment he saw car lights outside, and then Fay, with David behind her, came up the verandah steps and the first thing she did was to reach up and kiss Red. Martyn turned away, a feeling of burning jealousy in her heart.

Once greetings were over, Poppy disappeared into the kitchen for coffee. David gravitated towards Martyn, who had remained in her chair, and Fay flung herself down in a lounger exclaiming, 'Do you know we came across some blacks camped in the mulga, Red? On *our* land – with a fire lit and looking absolutely horrifyingly primitive. It shouldn't be allowed – I'll be simply scared to ride around by myself, they look really wild.'

'I don't think you need worry,' Red said laconically. 'They're a harmless lot – some of them are from round the station here and the rest would be relatives. You've got to remember they owned the land before we did, and though they're fast losing their old ways and their old freedom, there are still traditions and laws that hang on.'

David, who had dropped down on the floor at Martyn's feet and was leaning back against her legs, said lazily, 'The old walkabout thing. Always seemed lunatic to me. Personally, I don't favour employing staff who disappear when the spirit moves them. It's just too facile an excuse for not working.'

'It's hardly a problem,' Red said levelly. 'From my angle, I wouldn't interfere. You just learn to work with it ... If they scare you, Fay, keep out of their way, that's all.'

Poppy had brought the coffee, and Martyn, tiring of David's closeness and irritated as well as embarrassed that he had begun to stroke her bare ankle, got to her feet to hand round the cups.

'I should be able to go where I choose,' exclaimed Fay autocratically. 'Jindi-yindi belongs to me and David, after all. And the way they call me Fay – *blacks* whom I've never set eyes on in my life before, I'll swear. It's unnerving. And they *laugh* – at nothing. I never had this experience when Lewis and Aunt Ann were at Jindi-yindi – never!'

'That's not surprising,' Red commented, stirring sugar into his coffee. 'You didn't rove around in those days. You were over here in the daytime and safe at home with Lewis at night.' Martyn looked at him quickly, but his face was quite expressionless, and suddenly the subject was changed when David suggested a picnic the following day.

'Sorry, not for me,' Red said. 'You're welcome to stay the night if you wish, but I shan't be free tomorrow.'

Fay, her cup half-way to her lips stared at him suspiciously, and then looked at Martyn in a hostile way as if she might well be to blame. 'Why? What's on?'

'I'm driving to town to fetch Iris and the baby home.'

'Iris?' Fay repeated blankly.

'Drummer's wife,' Red said briefly.

Martyn's eyes shone. 'And the baby – Tancred?' she exclaimed impulsively.

'Sure,' he agreed with a grin. 'My namesake.'

Fay looked daggers. 'My God! What a cheek, to call the baby after you! But surely they can come out with the mail or something. You don't have to go, Red – not on a Sunday when you work every other day of the week and

144

it's the only time we get a chance really to see you.'

'Iris is special,' Red said, narrowing his eyes. 'Remember her, Fay? She used to work in the house here sometimes – a pretty, graceful girl—'

'None of them are *that*,' Fay protested, and though she smiled it didn't reach her eyes. 'Anyhow, I wish you'd change your mind, Red, just for once.' She turned to Poppy, whom she had more or less ignored. 'Red tells me Jan's getting back on her feet again, Mrs. Diamond.'

'That's right. All too soon she'll be married and I'll have the last of the girls off my hands. It makes me feel just a little bit sad. I'm sentimental, I suppose. But we'll make it a lovely wedding.'

'I'm sure you will,' Fay said politely. 'You'll be leaving us soon to make the arrangements. And you'll be going too, Martyn,' she added sweetly, turning her champagne-coloured eyes in Martyn's direction. 'I guess you've had almost enough of the outback by now. It's a lonely place, isn't it?'

'Lonely – but lovely,' said Martyn composedly, to her own surprise.

'Hardly lovely,' protested David. 'I'd prefer to live closer to the coast any time. Still, when you're left a property you don't turn up your nose at it. And if we hadn't taken it up, I'd never have met Martyn Verity,' he concluded, pulling the chair he had taken closer to her.

Martyn ignored the compliment which had sounded so insincere to her ears that it made her writhe, and when Poppy gathered up cups and tray and murmured something about seeing to the extra beds, she went to help her. The house girls were by now off duty, and once the rooms had been prepared for the unexpected guests, Martyn slipped off to her bedroom, and gave herself a too early – and consequently rather restless – night.

When she got up in the morning, Red had gone and her heart sank. She had had some totally illogical and unfounded idea that he might ask her to go along with him to collect Iris and the new baby. Her spirits sank lower

still when she discovered that *Fay* had gone with him –
though David was still around. She suffered all that day
from a burning jealousy, at the very thought of Fay alone
with Red. Just as though *she* had ever had any right to
him – just as though she hadn't known from her very first
day here practically, that Fay was head of the line for
being the future Mrs. Tancred Diamond. Her feelings
were so acute that she felt positively ill, so much so that
Poppy commented on her pallor. It served at any rate as
an excuse for rejecting David's suggestion that they
should go down to the swimming hole that morning. And
once breakfast was over, she retired to her room, where
for some time she looked over her drawings with a feeling
of dissatisfaction, and wondered when the ache in her
heart would go.

Never, seemed the most likely answer.

After lunch the three of them, David, Poppy and
Martyn, went out to the waterhole. It was cooler out
there, but for Martyn the two hours they put in were
scarcely tolerable. She was so utterly miserable and could
think of nothing but Red and Fay Bower. He was spending the day – the *whole day* – with her! But wasn't
he going to spend the whole of the rest of his life with
her, very probably? It hardly looked as if he were having second thoughts now, though last night she hadn't
thought Fay had showed up in very glowing colours. Red
must be pretty tolerant – or else his affair wasn't as
cold-blooded as he had made it appear. This time, Martyn
reflected moodily, his glasses were at least slightly rose-
tinted. And Fay must be really mad about him to have
made the trip today, seeing she'd have to come all the
way home in the car in the company of an aboriginal
woman with a little black baby named Tancred! The
thought made Martyn smile to herself – and her smile
provoked David's curiosity. She hoped she would be
able to see that piccaninny before she left Diamond
Springs . . .

She saw him that evening, after they went back to the

homestead. Red and Fay had already returned and were sitting in the garden in the shade of a big gum tree, smoking and drinking iced beer. Once again hot jealousy flared in Martyn so that she could scarcely bear to see them together. It would be a good thing when she and Poppy had left Diamond Springs. Poppy was walking ahead, while she and David brought up the rear, his arm possessively about her waist. Well, who cared? She let it stay there. She had been moody and silent all afternoon, and David had been fed up with her unco-operativeness, she was aware.

She slipped away as soon as she could to change out of her swim suit, and rather defiantly got into beige shorts, her sea-green top, and long socks – the very gear she had been wearing the first time she ever saw Red. Then, instead of going back to join the others, she went round the verandah, made her way through the back garden and down to the small cottage where Drummer and his family lived.

Iris – and she *was* pretty, as Red had said, with big cheekbones and lovely dark eyes – was sitting on the verandah nursing her baby, the pup Noosa was in the dust – wrestling with a large potato today! – the two little girls were admiring their baby brother, and Drummer sat nearby smoking a cigarette and looking very proud. The children were too shy to speak to Martyn, but Drummer got up to welcome her and invite her to come and see the baby.

'This Martyn Red tell you about,' he explained to Iris, and Martyn wondered what on earth Red had been saying about her. She stepped up on to the verandah, and Iris raised her big darkly lashed eyes and told her, 'We call him Tancred after Red. Next baby, mebbe Martyn after you. You fished those kids out of the river.'

So that was what Red had told her! Martyn smiled. 'Oh, it was nothing. Red did most of it anyhow.' Then she admired the baby, agreed that he was like Drummer, and that he looked 'plenty clever', and was about to go when

147

Red arrived.

'It's a fine big healthy baby, isn't it? I thought I might possibly find you here. Are you ready to come and join the company now? No more slipping away being anti-social like you did last night.'

She bit her lip and they walked back to the homestead together. Her feelings were mixed, just to be with him was both marvellous and unnerving. She had the feeling that the moment they rejoined the others, he and Fay would announce their engagement. 'Maybe they'll make it a double wedding with Jan and Barry,' she thought, and she longed to run away – to disappear.

'Did you have an enjoyable day?' he asked after a minute or so during which they had walked in complete silence. In the distance, Martyn could hear Noosa barking, and then the baby let out a lusty bellow. She glanced up at Red with a slight smile, but he had no answering one. 'I suppose you amused yourself very well with David.'

'That's right,' she agreed, wounded by his sharp-edged silver-grey look that was so impersonal.

'Yet I gather from Poppy that you've worked out your destiny and decided Bastian Sinclair is the man for you,' he said reprovingly. 'You're making a big mistake, you know. And quite frankly I find it hard to believe he actually wants to marry you, beautiful though you are. I'd have been prepared to bet one of my prize beasts that his proposition was a very different one.'

The colour surged into her face and she turned her head quickly aside. 'You always like to be right, don't you? Well, it's a pity, but you're not.'

'I'll make another bet, though. I'll bet you never do marry him.'

'You can bet whatever you like,' she said. They had come within sight of the others now. The blood had receded from her cheeks and she felt more composed and was able to look at him again. 'I don't care terribly much *what* you bet, Red Diamond.'

His gaze moved to her mouth and he smiled a little. 'No? I could make you care – about a lot of things – if I wanted to, Martyn Verity.'

'You think,' she retorted, and wished she could control her heart. He was so right – all the time – and if he once more got her into his arms she would be absolutely and utterly lost.

His eyes flicked over her. 'Why did you get back into the little girl gear today?'

'Perhaps because I am a little girl,' she suggested, annoyed. Was there nothing about her he could just leave alone?

'Oh no. I'll admit you can get away with it, but you're way beyond the little girl stage these days. You've grown up quite considerably since you came outback ... I'm sure David's senses will be titillated when he sees you in that get-up. I shouldn't like to be in Bastian Sinclair's shoes, quite frankly – with you out here playing havoc with all the available male hearts.' The last was said almost under his breath, for now they had reached the others.

Martyn's nerves were screaming. She moved quickly away from him and took a chair near Poppy. It was sheer torture to sit there while the others talked and she expected every moment to hear that Red and Fay were engaged.

Dinner was no better and yet eventually it was all over. Nothing had been said about engagements, and the visitors were actually on their way. At the last moment David, in full view of the others, took her in his arms and kissed her. She felt as little as if she had been a stuffed dummy – quite insensible – but over David's shoulders she saw Red, eyes narrowed, lips curling contemptuously. And then he turned away. To Fay.

# CHAPTER NINE

RED hadn't gone when she came out to breakfast next morning, though he was on the point of leaving. She had got into some of her new clothes – her honeymoon clothes – a particularly smart tailored cotton top, dark blue with a silky stripe in emerald green to match the very superior pants that went with it. It was a sort of morale-booster, because her morale had been very low during a restless, almost sleepless night.

Finding Red still about was unnerving, yet at the same time her heart leaped exultantly. He had already breakfasted and Poppy had gone to the kitchen for more coffee for Martyn when he appeared on the verandah where Martyn sat alone at the table. She glanced up and felt her face crimson, and saw his obviously amused reaction to that.

He said coolly, 'Waterbaby clothes are out today, I see. Who's the super-sophistication in aid of? You didn't know *I'd* still be around, did you?' She hadn't answered when he went on abruptly, 'Why don't you ride over to the muster camp this afternoon and we can come home together.'

She stared at him, stupefied. He, Red Diamond, was inviting her to the muster! And to ride home with him! She must be dreaming – she positively must! Or else she'd misunderstood somehow.

She said instinctively, without thinking it through, 'No, thanks. You might think I was chasing you.'

For an instant he looked quite baffled, and then he frowned and said quietly, 'I'm inviting you, Martyn.' His eyes, diamond-hard, bored into hers.

'And I'm – refusing,' said Martyn, quaking inwardly, and hoping he didn't know what an effort it cost her to refuse. An immense effort!

'Time's running out,' he warned, eyes glinting.

Her heart leaped like a startled deer. Wasn't *that* something she knew with every fibre of her being? Time was running out. Martyn Verity, who had come here a raw, innocent girl, would soon be leaving with a new maturity – admitted to by Red – that had cost her the price of a broken heart . . . Quickly she pulled herself together.

'If you mean what I think you mean – that I should see all I can of the outback while I'm here – well, I've already seen a fair bit. All I want to see.'

He leaned back casually against the verandah rail, a lock of dark hair falling across his brow, those shoulders that were so powerful and muscular straining against the material of the dark checked shirt he wore.

'Are you trying to tell me you don't like it here? That you've only been pretending—'

'Have I pretended? I thought I told you I preferred the sea.' She wished that Poppy would come back and break up this tête-à-tête – and yet too, she wished that she wouldn't. These days, in fact, she didn't know what she wanted at all. To spend twenty-four hours of the day in Red's company or not to see him at all. Each in its own way would be torture . . . 'Anyhow, I *belong* to the coast,' she said a little desperately. 'It's – it's nice enough out here – it's different—' Her glance went past him to the sunlit plain that stretched out and out beyond the garden. 'But the sea – the sea is my first and last love,' she concluded, conscious of her own artificiality.

His brows tilted cynically. 'That sounds really great. Most impressive. Rather like a line from some corny soap opera.' He paused. 'In other words, it's completely meaningless – empty words. Because one day when you're past the romantic first-love stage – if we can call it that – you'll forget all about the sea. You won't care, in fact, what landscape lies outside your bedroom window,' he concluded deliberately.

Her lashes came down defensively and her cheeks flamed. *That* had happened already, if he only knew it. If the truth were told, all she ever wanted to see through her bedroom window was what she was seeing right now ...

To cover up her discomposure she told him, 'I'm not in the romantic first-love stage anyhow. The man in my life is – mature—' She faltered, and to her relief Poppy came through the door with the coffee.

Five minutes later Red, with no further mention of his invitation, had gone.

The morning dragged by somehow, and Martyn was torn with a searing indecision. Would she ride out to the muster camp? It was a terrible temptation. He *had* invited her – but why? That was what she couldn't follow. Was it to tempt her – to see how she'd react? Because he refused to believe in her love affair with Bastian? – and how rightly! Because he had bet she would never marry Bastian? Or should she calm down and take it all at its face value? He was just offering to show her a little more of the outback. Quite likely she was making mountains out of molehills, looking for significance in something that was quite without it.

Mid-afternoon saw her down at the saddling yard, with Bob obligingly saddling up a horse for her and telling her casually, 'Yeah, the boss said you'd probably be wanting a horse. You're to have New Copper now, he said.'

New Copper was a little chestnut, and though she had little knowledge of horses it was apparent even to her that he was a finer horse than the one she usually rode, a bay. Perversely, she wanted to settle for the bay today, but the boss's orders were apparently to be obeyed – there was simply no question of Bob's being interested in her personal desire. So New Copper it was, and soon she was riding down one of the tracks that radiated from the homestead, under a blue and cloudless sky.

She told herself she was just taking a ride, that she wasn't going to take up Red's invitation, but she didn't really trust herself. When she came to a gate and had a choice of two ways to go, she chose the way that would, at least, take the longest time to get to the muster camp – *if* she should finally decide to go there. Almost by instinct, she headed in the direction that led to where she had seen the emus and chicks, and when she reached a certain clump of trees, she dismounted indecisively and walked her horse through bright sunlight and shadow, her hat hanging down her back, her blue and green shirt opened a couple of extra buttons to keep her cooler.

Presently a movement on the bright sunlit plain caught her eye. A horse and its rider were coming briskly in her direction. For just a moment her heart stood still, as she wondered if it were Red. But instinct told her it was not, and she hoped it wasn't David. Eventually it turned out to be Fay Bower – the Bower Bird – on a well-bred, high-spirited horse – that had no doubt cost a high proportion of the money that should have gone towards the re-stocking of Jindi-yindi. Fay rode beautifully, like a girl from a high-class riding school. She looked poised, sophisticated, and very sure of herself, and as well groomed as her horse – cream shirt, tobacco-brown riding breeches, shiny dark tan boots, on her head a soft cream felt hat with a plaited snakeskin band and chin strap. Ros had tried to equip Martyn adequately for the outback, but riding breeches and boots had not come into her calculations because Ros just hadn't reckoned on Martyn's taking up riding.

Fay reined in when she reached the trees, dismounted, tossed her reins carelessly and with a practised hand over a branch, and came towards Martyn.

'Hello. Where do you think *you're* going?' was her insolent greeting.

Martyn's chin went up. 'Why?' she asked flatly.

Fay coloured brightly with anger. 'I suppose you're planning to run down Red at the muster camp. Why can't you be satisfied with collecting just one scalp in the outback?'

'I don't know what you're talking about,' said Martyn.

'No? You've got David at your feet – but you want Red too.'

The two girls looked at each other with hostility. Martyn didn't think she had David at her feet, and she was sure Fay didn't think so either. As for Red – she was worried about him quite needlessly.

'So if you're chasing my man,' breathed Fay, '*don't*. Aren't you aware that Red and I are going to be married? If you aren't, then I'm telling you, and you might as well accept the fact and save your energy.'

Martyn felt herself trembling, partly from shock at Fay's – announcement, partly from the way in which the other girl addressed her. As if she hated every smallest bone in her body, every cell ... She said in a voice that was far from steady, 'Don't worry, I'm not chasing – your man, I'm – I'm looking for emus.'

Fay uttered a disbelieving exclamation and Martyn, who had had enough, turned her back, mounted New Copper as skilfully as she could manage – which was certainly not very skilfully – and cantered off. Fay called after her spitefully, 'Red won't be pleased to see you mishandling one of his best horses, I warn you!'

Martyn didn't bother to answer. It might have given her pleasure to tell Miss Bower that Red had left instructions that she was to have this particular horse, but she didn't come back to do so. Because she disliked Fay too much. And that, she admitted to herself as she gave New Copper his head and let him carry her out of the shade and into the heat of the burning sunlight, was completely and stupidly irrational. Fay was just a normal, likeable young woman. She must be, or Red wouldn't be marrying her. And *that* of course was the reason why Martyn hated her so much. Martyn's heart felt torn to shreds. It hurt her almost physically that Red was going to give his love – his passion – to Fay Bower. Yet it was going to happen, and even though she had more than half expected it, the fact was unbearable, searing.

She let New Copper go where he would, and then,

when they reached more trees, she reined in and tried to think rationally. But she discovered she was beyond rational thought. She was quite simply filled with a burning determination to go to that muster camp – to see Red – no matter who he was going to marry, and no matter what Fay Bower said. She sat quite still in the saddle, breathing evenly and trying to decide which way she had to go. Fay and her horse were not to be seen anywhere. In fact, there was no moving creature in sight, not even an emu, except far off across the plain, so far as to seem unreal, a few cattle moving slowly and feeding in the shade.

At this moment Martyn knew herself filled with the same compulsion that had made her swim out into the Pacific Ocean in pursuit of Red Diamond, weeks ago. *Then* she hadn't known what possessed her, what had driven her. Now she suspected it was the same emotion she was feeling now – that even at that early stage she must have responded to Red's attraction, at some level way below the conscious one. *Now* she admitted to physical attraction and to a whole lot more. She had fallen in love with Red Diamond, so madly, so helplessly that nothing else mattered – nothing. She had thought not so long ago that she would most assiduously avoid him for the rest of the time she was at Diamond Springs, but now she knew that she wouldn't. That she couldn't. Despite Fay, despite everything, she had to see him – to be with him – all she could. Pride was forgotten.

Eyes narrowed against the glare, Martyn chose her way unerringly. She touched New Copper's side gently with her knees, pulled lightly on the reins, and they were away off across the red plain with its covering of spiky grass clumps and near-green, after-flood growth.

Her mind went briefly to Stan. What would he have thought to see his daughter thus possessed by love – riding dementedly after a man who was going to marry another girl? To know that his daughter hungered to have that man's hands on her body, and his mouth against hers? A brief pang of shame struck through her, but she knew she had progressed far beyond the rough moral guidance that Stan had handed out. Love – passion – whatever you liked to call it – such as she harboured for Red Diamond put her way outside the influence of decent homely morals such as Stan had preached. This was – the law of nature, she supposed, and she felt her lips and her cheeks burning as she rode on.

She didn't know what she expected from Red. All she cared was that she should find him. He could lacerate her with his tongue – he could take a stockwhip to her. She would pay any price for a few moments of being real to him. His invitation of the morning now seemed no more than a challenge. He would not really expect her to come – not her, Martyn Verity.

But Martyn Verity never got even as far as the next paddock. Deep in thoughts that were driving her crazy with their insistence, she urged her horse away from the track to cut through long grasses that skirted a group of dark-leafed belahs, and suddenly – suddenly – right under New Copper's feet an emu rose up with a grunt and a hiss. The startled horse bucked and bolted, and Martyn was thrown clean out of the saddle. She hit the ground with a thud and every atom of wind was knocked out of her body.

She lay there unconscious, a crumpled heap in the long grasses. She didn't know that the emu, with a warning grunt to the chicks he had been sheltering in the sun, sauntered over curiously to look down at her; to stoop his long neck and methodically, though not very neatly, pick every button except one from her pretty blue and green shirt. And then, after another long stare from his double-lidded eyes, to return to his small family and bustle them off across the plain in search of another place where they could rest in the heat . . .

When at last her lids fluttered up, she saw nothing but an intense and unending blueness. Her body felt weightless, curiously numb and non-existent, and for a while she thought she had been killed. She thought she could see waves rolling in to the beach and seagulls flying, and she saw her father, Stan, his leathery skin, his wise and kindly blue eyes. And then she moaned because there was a fire in her breast. With an effort she moved one arm and discovered painfully that she had not been killed after all. The sea, the gulls, and Stan's face disappeared, and a shadow came across the blue of the sky.

A man with dark glinting eyes was stopping over her.

'For God's sake, are you all right?' Red Diamond asked.

Martyn struggled to sit up, groaning at the pain she felt. Instantly he had an arm around her to support her, then to lower her to the ground again. 'Stay where you are and tell me, if you can, what's happened – what's hurt you.' His voice was sharp, his eyes had narrowed to slits that glittered frighteningly. 'Has David Bower been here?' His fingers were pulling the edges of her shirt across her breast, and widening her eyes she saw that her blouse was completely unbuttoned. She stared with bewilderment. What *had* happened? For a moment her mind was completely blank and then remembrance came flooding back.

'The horse – New Copper – threw me. I'm – I'm all right.'

'Lie still,' he commanded when she tried to sit up again, and she obeyed weakly. His fingers were examining her now, gently, competently searching for broken bones. Her ankles, her legs, her ribs, her collarbone – she could feel those brown fingers on her bare skin. Then he was saying, 'You appear to be all in one piece. I'm going to get you out of the sun. Now just relax—'

His arms were around her as he lifted her from the ground, and she winced a little. There were no bones broken, but her body felt shocked right through, sore and bruised, and her ribs hurt when she breathed deeply.

'You were lucky to be cushioned by the grass,' he said close to her ear. This time when he held her she couldn't feel his heart beating, but she was aware of the dull shocks that shook her body as with long careful steps he carried her to the utility and settled her gently on the seat. She leaned back, closing her eyes, feeling perspiration break out on her forehead and upper lip. Automatically her hands went to her blouse, but when she tried to fasten it, the buttons weren't there.

Her eyes flew open and she met his hard quizzical gaze. As though it were a curious dream, she remembered his saying to her, 'I'm not going to turn a blind eye if you come home with half your buttons missing.' Now – it was just a little bit funny, but *all* her buttons were missing – all except one, and she knew exactly what he thought, and she knew— Of course! It was all coming back. The emu – hadn't Drummer warned her long ago of disturbing an emu in the long grass? And she had ridden blindly, carelessly, because she had been thinking so absorbedly of Red. Who now thought the worst of her . . .

He told her carefully, 'I came to look for you when New Copper came trotting up riderless. And I want to know – was David Bower with you before you took that fall? If so, I'll hunt him up and I'll—'

She stared at him wildly. Uncontrollable tears had welled up in her eyes and were spilling over. 'No, Red, it wasn't that at all.' She stopped, remembering Fay, and a pain struck through her heart. She had forgotten what Fay had told her, and now it was a new torture to look at the dark-faced man who stood by the open door of the utility and was reaching into the glove box. He took out a flask, unstoppered it, and held it to her lips without speaking. Martyn took a swallow and spluttered. She closed her eyes and hoped he wouldn't see her weak tears. She heard the car door shut, and then she sensed him getting into the seat beside her. The motor started up and the utility began to move slowly across the paddock.

'I'll get you home,' he said as if from far off. 'We'll have this out later.'

Martyn hardly remembered getting back to the homestead. Everything had become rather hazy. She knew that Red carried her to her room and that someone got her out of her clothes and into her old striped pyjamas. She remembered drinking some hot milk laced with some sort of spirit, and after that she supposed she slept.

When she woke again, the room was nearly dark and she could hear voices on the verandah. Red was saying something about 'shock'.

'She'll be about as good as new tomorrow.'

'About? What do you mean?' asked Poppy's voice. In her room. Martyn struggled to sit up and, wincing, reflected that *she* knew what he meant. She was going to be covered in bruises. But her head, fortunately, felt almost perfectly clear.

'Are you sure there's no concussion?' Poppy asked, the words sharp with anxiety.

'Pretty sure. I'll have a talk with her when she wakes and see if there are any signs. If there are, then of course she must go to hospital.'

Martyn discovered she was listening to his voice but hardly taking in what he said. That voice – would she ever be able to forget it? It was like Red himself. You couldn't say it was a beautiful voice any more than you could say he was a good-looking man. It was just – Red. Tough and masculine and uncompromising. And she, Martyn, loved it, and she loved his eyes and his hair, and the way his jaw was dark in the evenings, and she loved his big strong-fingered hands, and his broad shoulders, and his very toughness and maleness.

And all of it – *all of it* – was for Fay Bower.

She leaned across and switched on the bedside light, and almost instantly he – not Poppy – came through the verandah door into her room. She felt her breath catch in her throat just to see him.

'Well?' He looked at her from six feet away. His jaw was dark, he hadn't shaved this evening, she noted, her eyes taking him in from the cover of her lashes. He still wore the dark checked shirt and narrow trousers he had worn that morning, though that morning now seemed a lifetime away.

'Well what?' she asked, leaning back on the pillows, modest in her neat unfussy pyjamas.

'Have you recovered?' he asked dryly.

'Yes, thank you.'

'Any headache?' He came further into the room and sat on the side of the bed, his eyes looking at her searchingly.

'No. I didn't fall on my head.'

'You didn't exactly fall on your feet either, did you? Do you remember what it was all about? We hadn't finished talking, and now you're rested. I asked you if David had been around—'

'I told you no.'

'So you did. But I doubt whether it was a true answer. It's puzzling me what made you go galloping off at such a mad pace that New Copper threw you. And blouse buttons – let's face it – don't fly off of their own accord. Not in those quantities.'

She crimsoned. 'I wasn't galloping off anywhere. It was an emu – Drummer told me to watch out, but I forgot. It got up from the grass so suddenly – New Copper took fright—'

'I see.' He said it half abstractedly, his eyes watchful. Not – trustful, she thought wretchedly. 'And now, to return to the matter of your shirt,' he continued conversationally. 'How do you explain that away?'

She looked back at him unblinkingly. 'I suppose the emu could have picked off the buttons.'

He looked at her incredulously, his lips twisting cynically. 'You think I might believe that?'

She felt despair. She saw quite plainly that he had convinced himself she and David had been – wrestling, or making love or something. Well, she couldn't force his belief, but it was infuriating. She flared, 'Yes, I thought you might. Anyhow, does it matter all that much?'

'Yes, it does,' he grated. 'You're my stepmother's guest

160

and more or less under my protection while you're here, and I don't hold with rough love games being played on my cattle station. No matter what goes, down at the coast,' he finished brutally.

'You have a nasty mind.' Her voice shook a little. 'I'm not like that. And I'm not a liar either.'

It was a relief when Poppy appeared in the doorway bringing a tray loaded up with supper for Martyn – tea, creamy scrambled eggs, bread and butter. She deposited it carefully on the bedside table, and Martyn dashed away the angry tears that had come to her eyes, and wondered how much her hostess had heard of their rather heated discourse.

'Are you all right, Martyn?' Poppy asked. 'I should hate to send you home not completely whole.'

Martyn caught Red's eye and his caustic expression made her fume inwardly.

'I'm perfectly whole.' She added deliberately, 'It was just a fall. I'm a bit bruised, but otherwise fine.' To prove her point, she reached for the plate of scrambled eggs and began to eat.

'Should we let anyone know?' Poppy was still anxious. 'Your brother? Your boy-friend?'

'Just what were you planning to let her boy-friend know?' Red wanted to know, his eyes glittering unpleasantly. 'Don't meddle, Poppy. The girl's told you – she was tossed by a horse, she's bruised and shaken, but otherwise she's unharmed. Look at her! She's young, she's healthy – and she was lucky enough to fall in the nice soft grass.'

Martyn couldn't look at him. She felt her heart beating fast with anger, and for a second she had an impulse to bring the argument into the open. The thought struck her that Poppy must have noticed the mishap to her blouse when she was getting her to bed. *Poppy* would believe her story. She had parted her lips to speak when Red said dryly, as if aware of the direction her thoughts had taken, 'Poppy was down admiring Iris's baby when I brought you in. Otherwise she'd have tried to whisk you straight off to hospital. I think you'd sooner be here, wouldn't you?'

She couldn't answer. She lowered her head and continued eating her supper, though now it seemed tasteless. So Red had undressed her! It was the final indignity.

With a lazy movement, he rose from the bed.

'I'll leave you to enjoy your supper in Poppy's tender care,' he drawled out, and then he was gone.

She spent a couple of very quiet days after that. She didn't admit it to anyone, but the bruises on her shoulder and arm, the muscles of her back – all were painful. She wasn't up to riding or swimming, all she could manage was a bit of unenergetic walking. Down to see Iris and the children, out to the waterhole to see the birds. She had to have some exercise even if her shaken body would have preferred to remain supine. From the way Red avoided her, she was wretchedly convinced he didn't believe in her innocence.

Well, she supposed none of it mattered in the long run. He had never had what you would call a high opinion of her anyhow . . .

A couple of afternoons later he came home unexpectedly early. Martyn was sitting in the garden working up some sketches she had done of the children – largely in an attempt to give her mind something else to deal with besides the obsessive and unrewarding subject of Red Diamond. He crossed the lawn and looked over her shoulder, then took a nearby chair. He said, without even greeting her, 'I hope Bastian Sinclair will duly admire all the work you bring back – and be convinced that his innocent little paramour has spent her entire absence from him doing pretty drawings.'

Martyn flushed but said nothing. If he had come here simply to be unpleasant, then what was there she could do about it? – apart from packing up her things and going inside, and she simply wasn't Spartan enough to do that.

She had seen too little of him lately not to be grateful for his company in any circumstances.

She gave herself the pleasure of looking at him openly as he sprawled in his chair, his legs stretched out in front of him, his glittering eyes narrowed as they looked back at her. He hadn't showered, he hadn't shaved, he hadn't changed. He looked rough and tough and overpoweringly masculine with his heavy, broad-shouldered build, and she wondered how she had ever come to fall in love with him. How could any girl be in love with a man who treated her the way Red did Martyn Verity? He even thought she was a liar – he had absolutely no faith in her—

Neither of them said another word. They simply stared at each other for what seemed an eternity. She was on the point of breaking, of demanding what he wanted of her, when David Bower walked into the garden.

'Well, Red. Hello, Martyn, my cherry.' He stooped to drop a kiss on her forehead before she knew what he was about. Red's eyebrows descended, his mouth set in a hard line and he got up from his chair.

'Let's get into the office and discuss this business,' he said shortly. And in two seconds flat, Martyn was alone again.

Her peace of mind had completely disintegrated. She couldn't have cared less about her drawings. Her arms hung limply down, and she stared ahead of her, thinking, her heart leaden, 'Business. Jindi-yindi. And Fay.'

At last she stirred, dropped her sketchbook into her room, and walked through the garden and down towards the horse paddock. She had become fond of riding, but right now she couldn't have sat a horse as far as a hundred yards, her body had taken too much of a thrashing the other day. She simply walked – slowly, and she had no idea where. Anywhere to get away from her thoughts.

On the way back – it was just before sundown – she saw David's car rattling along the track towards her. As this was not the way to Jindi-yindi she had the feeling that he was looking for her, and she was right. He pulled up when he saw her, got out of the car and came towards her where she had paused under some trees. He had lost some of his civilized suavity, she thought, watching him come towards her. The thought somehow sprang into her mind that he'd been in a fight, and her heart quickened. Had he and Red been brawling? And if so, what about? Red had said they were going to talk business . . . Now she could see that one of his eyes was distinctly swollen, and she felt alarm. She had an impulse to turn about and run – an impulse, but not the strength. She wouldn't get far with her muscles in their present condition, and so she stayed where she was.

He stopped a few feet away from her. His amber eyes, one of them looking smaller than the other and marring his very good looks, were fixed on her almost menacingly.

'I was looking for you, little miss snake-in-the-grass Verity – just so I can tell you what I think of you.'

Martyn was taken entirely by surprise. Her head went up.

'Yes?' She hadn't the least idea what it was all about, knowing only that his attitude to her had changed drastically in the last little while – since he had called her 'my cherry'.

'You're a scheming little bitch, aren't you? – with your tinsel virtue, your spurious chastity. You've thrown a spanner bang into the dead centre of the works out here – and all with that innocent little-girl look on your face!'

Martyn's face whitened. 'I haven't the least idea what you're talking about – not the least.'

'No? What about the tales you've been telling Red about me behind my back? That I've been doing my best to rape you!'

'That's not true,' she breathed, frightened at what she saw in his face. 'I said – I said I hadn't seen you—'

'Then you didn't say it very convincingly. Besides which, I can't see there was any need for discussing me at

164

all. Well, if you will tell lies, I can pretty soon make them into truths.' He took a couple of steps towards her and she drew back. 'Right now, Red Diamond hates my guts, thanks to you. He's withdrawn his promise of the financial help we need on Jindi-yindi.'

Martyn heard him with a feeling of bewilderment. 'It has nothing to do with me. Didn't you – didn't you tell him there was nothing between us?'

He laughed briefly. 'When you got in first with your story, what would my word be? The damage was already done ... No, Miss Verity, your spit's blown back in your face this time – you'll find your lies have boomeranged on you.' His eyes ripped over her from head to foot as if they would tear her to pieces. 'God, what a little hypocrite! I bet you've been setting your cap at Red ever since you dropped down on Diamond Springs – I'll bet you came here with the express purpose of snaring him, even though that slippery stepmother of his must have told you he intended to marry my sister. You've certainly gone out of your way to make sure the Bowers are out of favour, haven't you?'

Martyn was shaking. No one had ever looked at her with such venom in his eyes before. Her heart quailed at what he must have told Red. Yet it was all so crazy! If he had denied it, everything would have been all right. Surely. It was absurd to think that Red would turn against the Bowers simply on her account. She said shakily, 'I've never set my cap at anyone. Not at Red – or you – or anyone. If you've told lies to Red about me—' She stopped because he had moved again and the expression in his eyes had intensified.

'Don't bother speculating,' he said between his teeth. 'I did. They were lies then, but they needn't stay that way. I'm going to dish out to you just what you deserve—'

Another quick step and he had seized hold of her and twisted her arms violently behind her back. She cried out in pain, and the tears rushed to her eyes. She was completely helpless as he kissed her in a way that made Bastian's kiss seem positively innocent. He had wrenched her arm, done violence to her stiff back, and the tears were running down her face. The next minute she was on the ground and he was crouching over her when a car screeched to a stop, and everything happened fast.

Red — it had to be Red! — hurtled out of the car, dragged David to his feet and dealt him a cracking blow on the jaw. Then with a strength and swiftness that seemed practically superhuman, he had swung David's unresisting body across the track and hurled it into the front seat of the car.

'Get going,' Martyn heard him rasp, as he slammed the door shut. He stood dark and threatening while the other man got the car going, and moved off erratically.

Only then did Red give his attention to Martyn. She had struggled to her feet and straightened her clothing, and she knew her face was ashen. Her whole body was trembling and though she had wiped the tears from her cheeks, her lashes were stuck together in points and her heart was thumping as though it would burst. Red's intervention seemed like a miracle, but now, as his diamond-bright eyes raked her over, she knew what he must be thinking and she was ready to crumple up and die.

He jerked his head. She had never seen his mouth set in such a hard and cynical line.

'Move. Into the car. I'll take you back to the homestead. It will be a good thing when you're back at the coast and someone else's responsibility. I see now why your brother was all too ready to hustle you off to the outback. Personally. I'm not going to concern myself over you any more — Bastian Sinclair may be just what you deserve.'

The sun had almost gone down, and the sky was flushed red. Reflected on Red Diamond's face it gave him the air of a terrible and powerful god — an avenging god. Martyn forced herself to move, though to walk, to keep herself upright, seemed to require an immense effort. She had almost made it to the car when she tripped over a tuft

166

of grass and all but fell. Red's arms caught her, his hand was against her fast-beating heart, and then he had whipped her around and she was in his arms and he was kissing her.

Violently at first – and then in a different way. So that from stunned unbelieving shock, she found herself carried into a different mood. She relaxed, melted, felt herself slowly absorbed into his being. The blood came back to her face, his arms supported her, and for a crazy moment she had a feeling of the utmost safety. Of more – of heavenly, peaceful bliss.

Then his mouth left hers and he released her slowly, and his eyes burned down into her face as she leaned back against the support of his iron-muscled arms.

'You melt against my body,' he said indistinctly. 'Your lips are honey – you could persuade me that to love you would be heaven ... But love's not a word you understand, is it?' His voice grew harsh, he chose his words with cold deliberation. 'As David Bower told me, you're a very willing little girl. I think I've been wasting my time getting angry over insults to your – virtue.'

To Martyn, the world seemed a crazy place. Red still held her firmly and though her bruises hurt, she was thankful, for otherwise she thought she would have slipped to the ground. Her eyes held by his, that flashed pinpoints of fire reflected from the flaming sky, she breathed out, 'I didn't want anything to happen with David. Can't you believe me? There's never been anything between us – and the other day, the day New Copper threw me—'

'David threw you first,' he said brutally, crudely, and she closed her eyes in shame. 'Oh yes, I checked with him on your story, and he wasn't in the mood for being gentlemanly and protecting your name. And to think that once I found you so modest – prudish, even!'

'He lied to you,' Martyn said huskily, a spot of bright colour in each of her cheeks. She thought that to die now would be good.

'*You* lied to me,' he said, unmoved. 'What sort of a girl are you? You responded even to me, just now. I wonder if you'd fall into the arms of any man who wanted you. My God, were you already like this when you came to Diamond Springs, or has it all happened since you've been in my care?'

'Your care!' she accused. 'You never cared what I did.'

'And did that matter to you?' he flung back. 'When you considered me the least likeable man you'd ever met?' He felt for cigarettes, and she took the last few remaining steps to the car and clambered in, mind and body agonized.

He didn't join her for several minutes, and when he came, it was almost dark. She was shivering with exhaustion and misery, but she made one more effort to clear herself.

'What happened just now – I couldn't stop David – he was angry because—'

'Don't protest, don't explain,' he said with a savage weariness. 'You're a strong girl. You could have evaded David Bower if you'd wanted to. You told me once – or have you forgotten? – that you'd fight for your virtue.'

'You forget I was hurt when New Copper tossed me the other day,' she flung back, angry now.

'I haven't heard you complaining,' he said with deadly coldness.

Martyn gave in. If he wanted to believe the worst of her, there was nothing she could do. Just now the fact that he was unjustly withdrawing his promise of financial help to the Bowers didn't seem to concern her. David had lied, but she didn't know why. The whole thing was an incomprehensible muddle. 'When I've left,' she thought wearily – and she hoped it would be soon – 'they can fight it all out amongst themselves.' Her body flagged.

# CHAPTER TEN

DINNER that night was an ordeal. Martyn had showered and changed when she came in. Her jeans and shirt looked disreputable and she thought, staring at her blanched face in the bedroom mirror, that Red had decided she was disreputable too, and it shook her to the core.

She wanted to weep, but that would have to wait till later on, when she was in bed with the long night ahead of her. Her morale had never been so low, and going back to Ros and Richard seemed like the promise of heaven. She looked at the two pretty dresses hanging in the wardrobe. Ros had imagined she might fascinate *someone* if she got herself dressed up. Well, she certainly hadn't fascinated anyone – on the contrary. In fact, she hadn't even put either of the dresses on, and she decided she would wear one of them tonight. To nail her colours to the mast, to prove to Red that she was not crushed, no matter what he thought of her.

She chose the one with the long sleeves; it was filmy, semi-transparent with a matching slip, and it would hide her shoulders and arms – she hadn't worn a sleeveless shirt since her fall. It was deep green in colour, with a low neck and a beautifully cut skirt that had a delicate floating quality about it. She slipped into it and knew that it became her very well, though the colour accentuated her unaccustomed pallor.

Certainly Red looked at her hard when she came into the dining-room – she had done a cowardly thing in missing out on the pre-dinner drinks – but Poppy looked at her too and remarked, 'You look lovely tonight, Martyn. Makes me feel guilty. We've never given you even the semblance of a party. I'm ashamed.'

Red added his comment. 'Quite the little mermaid,

aren't you, in your pretty green seaweed. Like someone out of a fairytale.' His eyes were cold and even Poppy looked puzzled.

Martyn smiled brightly as though everything was just marvellous, and took the chair that Red had pulled out for her when he rose. In her heart she wished she had stayed in her room on some excuse, but it was too late now. Besides, there would be tomorrow night, and the night after that – dinner every night with Red, until at last Poppy decreed it was time to go. And oh, God, Martyn prayed that that would be soon!

Red scarcely spoke to her during the meal. She had no appetite for once, and could only play with her food, good though it was. Poppy accused, 'You're not hungry, Martyn! Homesick for your boy-friend? Or aren't you feeling too peppy?'

She smiled palely. 'I do feel – just a little bit off colour. I'll go to bed early.'

'You must be leading a strenuous life lately,' Red said caustically. 'What have you been up to, I wonder?'

'Now, Red, Martyn had that nasty little accident the other day. She's probably still suffering from reaction. Isn't that it, Martyn?'

Martyn agreed that it was, and then Poppy went to get the coffee, leaving her alone with Red. She could feel his hard grey eyes examining her, and the colour came into her cheeks, but she didn't look up.

He said very softly, 'You are an extraordinarily beautiful young woman, Martyn Verity. More so than ever in that gown. You've blossomed from waterbaby to siren almost overnight. I guarantee a score of men will lose their heads over you in the years to come. Bastian Sinclair may have met his match in you after all – *he'll* be the one with the problems this time.'

Her blue eyes flashed up. 'And you don't mean that as a compliment, do you?'

'I think perhaps I do,' he said. And then Poppy was back. Martyn drank her coffee and excused herself.

She slept on and off in short snatches all through the night, waking again and again to lie and listen. Tonight she missed the sea – the friendly, ever-present sound of the sea. The silence of the outback had become strangely hostile. She listened tensely, her body rigid. There was no sound of emus drumming, no cry of owl or dingo, no rustling of leaves – no sound at all. She felt alone in the world, and the silence seemed a terrible kind of condemnation – a reality indissolubly mixed with nightmare.

Round about dawn, she left her bed and went on to the verandah in her pyjamas to look out across the garden and the plain beyond with weary, shadow-darkened eyes. The sky was paling, but the ghost of a moon still hung there, a mere silver wraith. The deathly silence had gone. Subdued sounds came from somewhere in the homestead, she could smell frying steak and toast, and she felt very hungry. Mrs. Hall was cooking breakfast for the men – and for the boss – before they rode out on the run for the day's work. Martyn stayed where she was for a long time, leaning against the verandah rail. She saw the long blue-grey leaves of the gum trees stir in the breeze that rose as the sun lifted itself out of the night, and she knew that despite everything there was a great deal of beauty – beauty that she hadn't even begun to discover – in the outback. She knew that she could become as enamoured of the plains, and this lonely, half harsh, half languorous country as she was of the sea, if she were ever given the chance. She had told Red once that the sea was her first and last love, but it had not been true then, and it was even less true now.

As she stood there, a line of horsemen began to move into her vision – the stockmen of Diamond Springs, wearing broad-brimmed hats, checked shirts, coloured neckerchiefs, all of them riding graceful and erect, most of them aboriginals or half-castes. One of them was different, and that one was Red Diamond. He rode erect too, he was dressed as the others were, but to Martyn's eyes there was something about his carriage that was un-mistakable, quite apart from the fact that he was a man of heavier build than any of the others.

Gazing at him then, her heart in her eyes, she had no idea that she was possibly seeing him for the last time. The knowledge was only imparted to her later.

Breakfast with Poppy, the usual inquiry – 'Did you sleep well?' And then, 'You look a bit washed out. I always forget that our outback heat can be devastating. You'll be glad to get back to the coast and your family and your boy-friend. Well, cheer up, Martyn, I have good news for you.'

Martyn felt a tiny warning shock in her heart, but Poppy didn't yet drop her bombshell.

'Eat up your breakfast and I'll tell you what went on while you were so peacefully asleep in your room last night . . . First of all, Jan rang up. Her wedding date's fixed and she wants me to come down as soon as possible and see to everything – the invitations, the dresses, the reception. Well, that suits me, I'm an organizing kind of woman, and I'll be in my element. We'll leave to-morrow,' she continued, and looked smilingly at Martyn as if she expected this would be the best possible news that she could give her. 'Are you pleased? I think you *do* want to get back, don't you?'

Martyn thought she would choke. Her appetite had vanished. Tomorrow! It was one thing to tell yourself you couldn't get away fast enough, it was quite another thing to know it was going to happen.

But Poppy hadn't finished yet.

'In the morning,' she said, 'Tancred's going to deputize one of the men to drive us in to pick up the feeder plane. He can't come himself – don't ask me why, but he's de-cided he has to camp out with the men tonight. I'm afraid it's not the best of good manners not to say good-bye to you, but he asked me to say it for you, and to wish you happiness.'

Martyn swallowed, and looked down at the table, sure

that the death of her heart must be there in her eyes.

'I hope the arrangements are okay with you?' Poppy asked brightly.

Martyn nodded. 'Of course. Whatever you plan,' she said huskily.

'Good ... I haven't any need to hang on here any longer, either. What I wanted to happen has happened.'

Martyn raised her blue eyes, puzzled. What had happened? Her expression asked the question for her.

'The Jindi-yindi Fay-Bower business has worked out satisfactorily – and I might as well have saved myself the bother of worrying about it.'

'What – do you mean?' Martyn managed to ask, jerkily.

Poppy buttered toast and bit into it with enjoyment.

'Red's dropped the idea of dedicating half his energies – and half his finances – to Jindi-yindi. And better still, he's dropped the idea of asking Fay to marry him.' Her dark eyes were narrowed and she didn't see Martyn's startled reaction. She had thought he *had* asked Fay to marry him! Poppy was smiling ironically. 'He's decided he's not interested in marriage after all. That having lived this long without a wife he can continue on indefinitely ... Ah well, he's discovered the truth of what I've been preaching for a long while – the weakness of the Bowers. Personally, I'm glad he's decided not to help David.'

'He – he told you why?'

'In detail. And he was ropeable! He had it all out with David yesterday. He says David just doesn't belong out here – he should go back east and buy himself a small going concern. I don't think it will hurt if I tell you about it – it's not as if you lived here.' Poppy reached for more coffee. 'Things have been going from bad to worse. David's said Yes to all Red's advice and never taken it – got his own fencing contractor and now he's been ditched with the work half finished; wouldn't buy store cattle when he could have got them dirt cheap – spent a fortune on horses, all for show. But what really brought things to a head was the fact he used the Diamond name – unauthorized – for credit at some cattle sales the other day – the day you had your accident, to be exact. And Red found out and called him to account. Yesterday.'

So, thought Martyn, a little dazedly, none of the fracas had had anything to do with her, no matter what David had said. And most likely, Red had never made David any promises at all.

'But – Fay?' she asked. 'Just because of David, he—'

Poppy shrugged. 'He didn't go into that. But isn't it proof that his heart wasn't involved? Well, she's probably feeling sorry for herself and badly done by, but it would never have worked. She's just not the type for Red. For instance, I've heard her say things about Drummer that would upset anyone. And Drummer has always had a special place in Red's affections. Those two have known each other practically all their lives and they've been through a lot together. Once, when they were teenagers, and Red's horse got into trouble in a flood river, Drummer saved his life.'

Breakfast was finished, but Poppy stayed on, reflective, content, and quite unaware of the turmoil in Martyn's mind. For Martyn, one fact stood out starkly amongst the others. She was never to see Red again. She was to leave in the morning without another glimpse of him. It was sheer agony – and far more real than the fact that he was not going to marry Fay.

Poppy said presently, 'This sleeping out at the camp – I don't like it. I've seen too many men break away from the little civilized decencies of life, gradually become misanthropes. It mustn't happen to Red, simply because he's been disillusioned by the Bowers. He should marry, and have the good life he's earned.' She was silent for a moment, staring out into the red-gold heat of the morning. 'Shall I tell you something, Martyn? It's a bit in the nature of a confession—'

Martyn supposed she must have made some answer, for Poppy went on, 'When I invited you here, it was because I wanted you and Red to marry.'

Martyn had known that, of course. She had also known there had been other girls, and no doubt Poppy had had high hopes of each of them. This time she had certainly made a mistake!

'When I saw you and Red together that first day at Julia's,' Poppy confessed, 'you just looked so absolutely right together. I don't know – so utterly beautiful. You so young and blonde and suntanned, Red so dark and masculine and powerful. I just had this utter conviction that you were the girl for him. I'm afraid the excuse I made about Jan was only an afterthought – and the fact you had a problem of your own. Oh, didn't I think I was clever! You hadn't told me about this boy-friend of yours then. I should have guessed there'd be someone else.' She smiled ruefully across at Martyn. 'It was an idea that went completely haywire, wasn't it? You two aren't attracted to each other even in the slightest degree.'

Martyn smiled back, but her heart was aching. Poppy was only half right. Red was not attracted to her – but she would die for him!

That morning she tidied out her room and did some washing, ready for her departure. It was while she was hanging her clothes on the line – and looking unhappily at the blouse with the buttons ripped off it – that a sudden thought struck her. She stood perfectly still. Poppy had said that David had gone to some cattle sales 'the day you had your accident'. Wouldn't *that* prove to Red that she hadn't lied to him? That she had not been with David before New Copper tossed her? She would put it to him anyhow, and at least try to clear her name.

And then she realized that she wouldn't have the opportunity. Red wasn't coming home tonight – most likely because he never wanted to see Martyn Verity again. She stood in the hot sunlight, her arms hanging limply by her sides, feeling futility, despair.

Then her head went up. She would ride out and find Red, force him to believe her . . . In her heart she knew it was merely an excuse to see him again, because there were other things he believed of her that were to her disadvantage – and basically, she wasn't going to change anything. All the same, she was going.

Over lunch, she told Poppy a half-lie.

'I'd like to have one last ride around. I may never visit the outback again. And if you would, could you show me the map of Diamond Springs again so I can be sure I've got my bearings?'

That was how she found out exactly where Red would be.

She took New Copper again, and mounted stiffly, newly aware of the bruises and stiffness in her body. She certainly wasn't going to get much physical enjoyment out of her ride, but if she was making a martyr of herself, it was because she wanted it that way.

The sun was hot on her back as she rode off, and though she glanced about her, determined to enjoy her last sight of this part of the country, she was too abstracted to delight in the sight of the shimmering plains, the sculptured shapes of the galahs, the flights of the birds. The only thing that roused her was the sight of two emus stepping it out together by a distant fence, their strange, hairlike feathers ruffled by the wind.

She thought she would find the camp quite easily. It wasn't very far – and that was why it was so meaningless for Red to be camping out for the night. There were two ways to choose from. The shorter way would mean a final ride across an open paddock in full view of the camp, and so she turned off at the appropriate place in favour of the second way. It took in a river crossing, but she would have the shelter of trees along the river bank while her eyes sought out Red and she waited for an appropriate moment to approach him. She knew the river had been rising in the last few days, but she hoped the crossing, that had been clearly marked on the map, would be negotiable.

At last she was riding through the trees by the river bank, following a narrow red track obviously used by horses rather than vehicles, and then there was a sharp little descent to the river. There she reined in her horse to make sure she wasn't asking for trouble. The river was the colour of milk coffee, and flowing fast. There were small eddying patches of foam here and there, and small bits of half-submerged debris spun by, further downstream there were rocks and the banks grew steep and the water looked deeper, and more treacherous.

New Copper appeared undeterred by the sight of the water, and Martyn urged him gently in. There were fresh hoofmarks on the track, and that was a good indication. She aimed for a little further upstream, to allow for the current, and that way felt certain of reaching the track where it emerged across the stream.

It was a piece of cake. The horse was confident and made the crossing without even having to swim, and without stumbling once, and in a few minutes was scrambling up the further bank.

Reaching the shelter of the trees, Martyn dismounted, tossed the horse's reins over a branch and walked forward to get the lie of the land. Some distance away she sighted a mob of cattle, some encircling stockmen and – Red. Her blue eyes, screwed up against the glare, found him almost instantly, and her heart leaped in recognition and joy. And then she recognized the rider of the horse reined in alongside him, to whom he was talking. A girl in a cream hat with a snakeskin band, immaculate in pale lemon shirt and dark riding breeches.

Fay Bower.

No longer riding that thoroughbred horse her brother had bought for her, but an ordinary stockhorse.

Martyn stopped dead in her tracks, pain in her heart where before there had been exhilaration and – she admitted it now – a mad hope. Those two sat their horses in the hot sun, utterly intent on each other. Red's wide-brimmed hat cast a deep shadow over his face, and of course from this far she hadn't a hope of reading his expression. She only knew those two were together again and that Poppy must have been wrong – or Red had been fooling her, for some reason of his own. He couldn't finish with Fay – the affair hadn't been heartless. At any rate, it must be on again or she wouldn't be there at his side, her back so erect, looking, even from this distance, so confident. And he, head inclined, was listening to her.

Martyn knew suddenly she had been an idiot to come racing out here. She might salvage a little of her pride in pointing out that she hadn't lied about David the day of her accident, but it would get her nowhere. Tomorrow she would still be on the plane heading for Sydney, while here in the outback – if Red Diamond wanted to, he could go ahead and marry Fay Bower. Hadn't Martyn heard him tell Poppy, 'Anything I do, you can be sure I do it because it's what I want to do?'

She turned away. And now it was not the sunlight that blinded her, but her own tears.

She walked under the trees. In a minute she would go back to New Copper. In a minute. Just now her body ached worse than ever, as if in sympathy with her heart. Though it was riding that had made her muscles ache in reality. And riding back, away from love and hope – foolish groundless hope – was going to be a very different matter from riding towards Red. Suddenly the homestead seemed too many miles away, the thought of sitting a horse all those miles quite intolerable.

She looked back through the trees. The girl from Jindi-yindi was no longer talking to Red. As Martyn watched, she touched her horse's flanks with her spurs and was suddenly flying across the paddock straight towards the trees where Martyn waited. Exhilarated, her hat flying off to hang down her back. How Martyn envied her.

'She's won him back,' she thought. If she had ever lost him.

The other girl didn't see her. Her horse charged madly through the trees a little way off and Martyn heard the clatter of stones as she took him at what was surely an insane pace down the bank. But surely she had made a mistake. She was too far downstream for the crossing. Martyn began to run through the trees in pursuit. Horse and rider had slithered right down the steep bank and now the horse seemed to be balanced precariously over the water and was whinnying in fear while Fay clung to its back.

Martyn called out, 'Fay, don't go in there – it's too deep! Come back!'

It was useless. The horse, that had been tottering on the brink, had suddenly plunged into the river. The water was deep and its nostrils flared with fright as it floundered, tossing its head up. Fay, even more frightened than the horse, pulled her feet free of the stirrups, and keeping hold of the horse's mane, slipped out of the saddle, no doubt with the idea of getting back to the bank. But by now they were well out into the stream and the horse lashed out in panic. Fay's hands lost their hold and the river swept her away. She went under, then surfaced, spluttering and coughing, while further upstream her horse, its eyes rolling, struggled on.

Even as it all happened, Martyn had slithered down the bank, pulled off her shoes and was in the water and swimming towards Fay. She saw the other girl being whirled on helplessly, and then she was flung towards the far bank where the rotten branches of an old tree showed menacingly above the water. She disappeared momentarily, then emerged choking, her arms flung out as she tried to grasp at something to hang on to.

Martyn called out, 'Hang on, Fay –I'm coming!' But she didn't know if Fay heard her or not.

Her jeans were heavy with water and her shoulders ached with every stroke she made. It seemed an interminable time till she reached the other girl, whose hands clawed at her desperately.

'My foot,' Fay croaked. 'It's caught – I can't get it free – help me – help me—!'

'Then let go of me,' gasped Martyn, all but winded with the effort she had made and in danger now of being dragged under by those clinging hands. She took hold of them and wrenched them away, then duckdived down into the muddy water.

Down there, she was in a world of almost total darkness. Fay's foot, in its riding boot, was tightly wedged between two branches. Using both her hands, Martyn pulled and twisted, cutting her fingers on the splintery wood. Then, just when she thought her lungs were about to burst and it was becoming absolutely imperative for her to surface again, she got Fay's leg free. Instantly the other girl kicked out and Martyn received a shove in the chest that made her gasp and take in a lungful of water.

It was a second before her reeling senses told her that something else was wrong. She should have been bobbing up to the surface now, but horror of horrors, something was holding her down, and with her last conscious thoughts she realized that the leg of her jeans was caught on a snag.

Then the blackness became total, everything was blotted out and all feeling left her.

She opened her eyes, and it was dark – pitch dark. She wasn't conscious of having a body. The water – her lips parted and she gave a little choked cry. There was no water. She stared into the darkness, and now it was darkness no longer. A small red glow moved and then stayed still. She heard a gentle click and a light came on – a soft light, though it still hurt her eyes so that she flinched and closed them momentarily, then opened them again.

Where was she? Her eyes wouldn't focus properly. She had been dreaming – having a nightmare. She had thought that Fay – that she—

She struggled to sit up and discovered that a blanket was wrapped closely round her from her neck to her feet.

'Martyn,' a voice said, and a hand reached out – brown, very solid and strong – to cover her shoulder again.

Her vision cleared. It was Red's voice, it was his hand, and now she was looking into his face. Impossibly, she was in her room at Diamond Springs. Tears came into her eyes and she sank back on the pillow again.

'What – happened?' she asked weakly.

His hand touched her hair. 'It's all over now. You're safe, quite safe.'

Her blue eyes stared at him. It was beginning to come back. She had been in the river – Fay had been trapped – she had tried to free her. Her eyes widened in an unspoken question.

'Everybody's safe,' Red said. 'Even the horse. Fay – you—'

'I thought I was going to drown. Fay must have saved me—'

He shook his head, his expression intensely grave. 'No, I saved you, Martyn. You're mine now.' He stood up. 'We'll talk about it later. I'm going to ask Poppy to see to your needs.'

She didn't want him to go. She wanted to ask him to repeat what he had said – something quite incredible. Or else her mind was wandering and he hadn't said it at all ... To detain him, she asked, 'What time is it?'

'A little after eight, that's all. You'll have a little supper if you feel up to it, and then you must sleep.'

'Because in the morning, I'm leaving,' she thought, as other memories flooded back. There was something she had wanted to tell him – about David. She said painfully, 'Red – that day New Copper threw me—'

He held up his hand. 'I know. David was at the cattle sales. I realized it this morning. I was coming back this evening to ask you to forgive me.' Suddenly he was kneeling by the bed and there was an expression in his eyes she had never seen there before. He said, huskily, 'Oh God, Martyn, do you know that I love you – that I love you more than life? If I'd lost you today the river could have had me too.'

Martyn closed her eyes. She felt hot tears on her cheeks and she knew that she must be dreaming.

Everything was vague after that. She didn't know if she slept again, but Poppy was there looking after her, feeding her chicken soup, bread and butter. She wasn't hungry, but she felt very tired.

'What happened?' she heard herself ask querulously.

'Red says you're not to talk any more tonight.'

There must have been something in the tea Poppy made her sip, because she was falling asleep again – deep into sleep, a sleep without dreams.

It was late when she woke in the morning, and what wakened her was the sound of someone in the room. It was Poppy, all dressed up as if she were going somewhere. Martyn suddenly sat up in bed with a feeling of guilt.

'Oh, it's time to go and I'm not dressed or packed up—'

'Re-lax,' drawled Poppy. 'I'm leaving you behind. You don't have a wedding to arrange – well, not someone else's,' she amended oddly. 'I just sneaked in to say goodbye. I promise I'll look up your brother and his wife and tell them that you're safe and well and – happy?'

Happy? Martyn frowned a little. And – well? Because hadn't she nearly drowned? But Red had saved her ... She said uncertainly, 'Couldn't you wait? I can be ready in a few minutes—'

'No hear,' said Poppy. 'Red would never forgive me. You can't just run away like that. And remember, Mrs. Hall is here.' She smiled, and stooping, kissed Martyn on both cheeks. 'I have to go. But I'm leaving you in good hands. Be seeing you!'

She was gone, and Martyn leaned back on the pillow thoughtfully. Her mind felt alert, and she thought it was time to sort out what was true from what she had dreamed last night. Red had certainly saved her from the river, and she knew that Fay was safe. But otherwise – she must have dreamed the things he had said.

Yet something insisted that she had not. That Red — loved her. It was nothing short of a miracle.

Suddenly she was terribly hungry.

She showered quickly and washed the river water from her hair. Then she put on the clothes she had been wearing when first she met Red — shorts, socks, a top that was deep-sea green, and that showed the fading bruises on her shoulder. It was a strange, back-to-the-beginning thing to get into that particular outfit. It seemed to wipe out all the in-between things, so that she could start again. With truths. About Bastian, for instance.

Mrs. Hall provided her with breakfast when she put her head around the kitchen door and said in a meek voice, 'Please — I'm so *hungry*!'

She ate on the wide back verandah where the men had their meals. She ate steak and eggs and toast, and drank gallons of tea. In the back yard she watched a cat stalking a magpie — a cat with a red bow on its tail and another round its neck.

'Who did that?' she asked Mrs. Hall, laughing.

'Oh, those kids of Drummer's. They're little mischiefs.'

The sun was shining — and no doubt it was broiling hot outside, and by rights she should have been on her way to the coast where there was always a cool breeze. But there was no doubt in her mind where she would sooner be. In the kitchen, Mrs. Hall was making bread and the dough was rising and Martyn was fascinated. She had the strangest feeling of freedom in the big kitchen that had, till now, seemed to belong to Poppy. Mrs. Hall was a friendly woman, and — at last she had to ask it or go mad.

'Where's Red?'

'Oh, he'll be in this evening. He left instructions that you were to have a lazy day. My, you were lucky he saw you in the river when he rode over to see if Fay had got safely across, weren't you?'

Martyn nodded. So that was how it had happened! She felt all on edge — a lazy day meant no riding, she would have to wait till evening before she could ask him why she was still here when Poppy had gone. Yet she knew why – though she couldn't believe it.

The day seemed endless.

When he came home, it was nearly sundown and she was on the verandah. She greeted him with a careful and deliberately schooled casualness – as though she remembered nothing of what he had said last night. Because – just possibly – she had dreamed it.

'Well, are you in your right mind again, Martyn Verity?'

'Yes.' She kept her face turned to his and tried to persuade herself that she wasn't flushing. 'I could have gone with Poppy this morning – I don't need to be kept – under observation—'

'No?' His brows rose quizzically. 'I contest that. What sort of a man would I be to let you go back to Bastian Sinclair when you made me a declaration of love yesterday?'

She stared at him blankly. She thought she had been blushing before, but now her cheeks were scarlet.

'I – I didn't,' she stammered.

'You did,' he said. 'In very plain words. Though I admit you were barely conscious. Is it true?'

She looked back at him, straight into those diamond-bright eyes, and there was something there that made it impossible to tell anything but the truth.

'Yes,' she said with the utmost simplicity.

'And I love you,' he said. 'Madly.'

He drew her into his arms and kissed her, and it was a kiss that was neither gentle nor fiercely passionate, but very, very possessive.

Of one accord they moved down from the verandah then, and into the garden, away from the homestead and the yellow lights that Mrs. Hall had switched on. His arm about her, he asked quietly, 'Can you forgive the unforgivable, Martyn? The things I've thought about you, and none of which, I would swear now, are true. Can you believe that, as far as David was concerned, it was sheer blind jealousy that made me go berserk and suspect what I did?'

They had paused under some loquat trees and she looked up into his face. 'I believe you. And of course I forgive you. But why did David lie?'

He shrugged. 'I guess he thought if I wasn't going to link up with Jindi-yindi and Fay, then he was going to make sure I didn't marry you, either. I'll admit I'd been thinking seriously of Fay – but I revised my ideas completely very shortly after you turned up at Diamond Springs.'

'Yesterday,' said Martyn hesitantly. 'Why was she there with you?'

'Oh, she'd come to tell me David had a buyer for his bloodstock horses and that he'd used my name as a temporary security only. It's something that needn't concern you – a sort of final effort to – bring me back into the fold.'

Poor Fay, Martyn thought briefly, and then dismissed her from her thoughts, because Red was kissing her again.

He said quizzically, 'I was right when I said you'd never marry Bastian Sinclair, wasn't I, mermaid?'

'I was never going to,' she admitted. One day she would tell him the whole of that story, but not just now.

'No? Wasn't that what you had in mind when you came outback? Wasn't that your personal problem?'

She shook her head. 'It was a career problem,' she said meekly. 'Ros and Dick want me to do a secretarial course and I don't—'

'Well, that's easily settled, isn't it?' he said, laughing.

Martyn smiled a little. She could just imagine Dick's and Ros's alarm when she told them she was engaged – despite Ros's wishful thinking when she had fitted her out with a honeymoon wardrobe and suitcase! 'Getting engaged? After you've been away less than a month? Who on earth is he? Now look here, Bit' – this would be Richard – 'you're positively not getting engaged or anything at all until we've met this man.'

And what would they think of him when they met him? Martyn couldn't see how they could possibly be anything but delighted. Stan would have been pleased. Because Red was everything a man should be – Red was just out of this world—

He asked her teasingly, 'Well, how do you think they'll react to our engagement, waterbaby?'

'They'll be mad about it,' she said, idiotically, sliding into his arms.

# THE
# OMNIBUS
## A GREAT IDEA FROM HARLEQUIN

# NOW AT RETAIL

Rosalind Brett

Eleanor Farnes

Iris Danbury

Amanda Doyle

Rose Burghley

READ ON FOR EXCITING DETAILS ...

# A GREAT VALUE!

Almost 600 pages of pure entertainment for the unbelievable low price of only $1.95 per volume. A truly "Jumbo" read. Please see the last page for convenient Order Coupon.

# Amanda Doyle

### A Change For Clancy (#1085)
Clancy hadn't liked the new trustee-appointed manager of Bunda Down, Jed Seaforth—but when Johnny Raustmann threatened him she somehow found herself emotionally involved.

### Play The Tune Softly (#1116)
Ginny's joy in her new job at Noosa was shattered when she found Jas Lawrence there—the one man she never wanted to see again.

### A Mist In Glen Torran (#1308)
There'd been many changes at Glen Torran, but Verona was dismayed to find Ewan MacKinnon still expected to inherit her along with his brother's estates.

# Iris Danbury

### Rendezvous In Lisbon (#1178)
Janice Bowen went into the impossible Mr. Whitney's office to resign. Instead, she found herself agreeing to accompany him on a business trip to Lisbon!

### Doctor At Villa Ronda (#1257)
Nicola usually ignored her sister Lisa's wild suggestions, but this time accepted her invitation. She arrived in Spain to find that Lisa had mysteriously disappeared.

### Hotel Belvedere (#1331)
Andrea took on a job at the luxury hotel where her aunt was head housekeeper, only to find her life becoming increasingly and dangerously complicated.

# A GREAT IDEA!

We have chosen some of the works of Harlequin's world-famous authors and reprinted them in the 3 in 1 Omnibus. Three great romances — COMPLETE AND UNABRIDGED — by the same author — in one deluxe paperback volume.

## *Joyce Dingwell* (2)

**The Timber Man (#917)**
It was bad enough to have to leave Big Timbers, but even worse that Blaze Barlow should think Mim was leaving for the wrong reasons.

**Project Sweetheart (#964)**
Alice liked being treated as though she were something special—she privately believed she was. Then Bark Walsh, the project boss, suddenly ended her reign!

**Greenfingers Farm (#999)**
It never occurred to Susan that circumstances were not as they seemed, and that her well-intentioned efforts as companion, were producing the wrong results!

## *Mary Burchell*

**Take Me With You (#956)**
Lucy fought hard for a home of her own—but it was her return to the old orphanage that provided the means to achieve it.

**The Heart Cannot Forget (#1003)**
Andrea didn't take Aunt Harriet seriously about inheriting her estate until she met her aunt's dispossessed and furious nephew Giles and his even angrier fiancee.

**Choose Which You Will (#1029)**
As companion to old Mrs. Mayhew, Harriet expected a quiet country life—but quickly found her own happiness at stake in a dramatic family crisis.

# HARLEQUIN OMNIBUS

A Jumbo Read !!!

## Elizabeth Hoy

### Snare The Wild Heart (#992)
Eileen had resented Derry's intrusion to make a film of the island, but she realized now that times had changed and Inishbawn must change too!

### The Faithless One (#1104)
Brian had called her love an interlude of springtime madness but Molly knew that her love for him would never quite be forgotten.

### Be More Than Dreams (#1286)
Anne suddenly realized her love for Garth was more important that anything else in the world—but how could she overcome the barrier between them.

## Roumelia Lane

### House Of The Winds (#1262)
Laurie tricked Ryan Holt into taking her on safari despite his "no women" rule—but found it was only the first round she'd won!

### A Summer To Love (#1290)
"A summer to love, a winter to get over it," Mark had once joked. But Stacey knew no winter would help her get over Mark.

### Sea Of Zanj (#1338)
A change of scenery, a little sun, a chance for adventure—that's what Lee hoped for. Her new job didn't work out quite that way!

# LOOK WHAT
# YOU MAY BE MISSING

### Listed below are the 26 Great Omnibus currently available through **HARLEQUIN READER SERVICE**

**Essie Summers #1**
Bride in Flight (#933)
Meet on My Ground (#1326)
Postscript To Yesterday (#1119)

**Jean S. MacLeod**
The Wolf of Heimra (#990)
Summer Island (#1314)
Slave Of The Wind (#1339)

**Eleanor Farnes**
The Red Cliffs (#1335)
The Flight Of The Swan (#1280)
Sister Of The Housemaster (#975)

**Isobel Chace**
A Handful Of Silver (#1306)
The Saffron Sky (#1250)
The Damask Rose (#1334)

**Joyce Dingwell #1**
The Feel Of Silk (#1342)
A Taste For Love (#1229)
Will You Surrender (#1179)

**Sara Seale**
Queen of Hearts (#1324)
Penny Plain (#1197)
Green Girl (#1045)

**Mary Burchell #1**
A Home For Joy (#1330)
Ward Of Lucifer (#1165)
The Broken Wing (#1100)

**Susan Barrie**
Marry A Stranger (#1034)
The Marriage Wheel (#1311)
Rose In The Bud (#1168)

**Violet Winspear #1**
Palace of Peacocks (#1318)
Beloved Tyrant (#1032)
Court of the Veils (#1267)

**Jane Arbor**
A Girl Named Smith (#1000)
Kingfisher Tide (#950)
The Cypress Garden (#1336)

**Anne Weale**
The Sea Waif (#1123)
The Feast Of Sara (#1007)
Doctor In Malaya (#914)

**Essie Summers #2**
His Serene Miss Smith (#1093)
The Master of Tawhai (#910)
A Place Called Paradise (#1156)

**Catherine Airlie**
Doctor Overboard (#979)
Nobody's Child (#1258)
A Wind Sighing (#1328)

**Violet Winspear #2**
Bride's Dilemma (#1008)
Tender is The Tyrant (#1208)
The Dangerous Delight (#1344)

**Rosalind Brett**
The Girl at White Drift (#1101)
Winds of Enchantment (#1176)
Brittle Bondage (#1319)

**Kathryn Blair**
Doctor Westland (#954)
Battle of Love (#1038)
Flowering Wilderness (#1148)

**Iris Danbury**
Rendezvous in Lisbon (#1178)
Doctor at Villa Ronda (#1257)
Hotel Belvedere (#1331)

**Mary Burchell #2**
Take Me With You (#956)
The Heart Cannot Forget (#1003)
Choose Which You Will (#1029)

**Amanda Doyle**
A Change for Clancy (#1085)
Play The Tune Softly (#1116)
A Mist in Glen Torran (#1308)

**Rose Burghley**
Man of Destiny (#960)
The Sweet Surrender (#1023)
The Bay of Moonlight (#1245)

**Joyce Dingwell #2•**
The Timber Man (#917)
Project Sweetheart (#964)
Greenfingers Farm (#999)

**Roumelia Lane**
House of the Winds (#1262)
A Summer to Love (#1280)
Sea of Zanj (#1338)

**Margaret Malcolm**
The Master of Normanhurst (#1028)
The Man in Homespun (#1140)
Meadowsweet (#1164)

**Elizabeth Hoy**
Snare the Wild Heart (#992)
The Faithless One (#1104)
Be More Than Dreams (#1286)

**Anne Durham**
New Doctor at Northmoor (#1242)
Nurse Sally's Last Chance (#1281)
Mann of the Medical Wing (#1313)

**Marjorie Norell**
Nurse Madeline of Eden Grove (#962)
Thank You, Nurse Conway (#1097)
The Marriage of Doctor Royle (#1177)

# *Harlequin Reader Service*

# ORDER FORM

**MAIL COUPON TO** ▶ Harlequin Reader Service,
M.P.O. Box 707,
Niagara Falls, New York 14302.

**Canadian SEND Residents TO:** ▶ Harlequin Reader Service,
Stratford, Ont. N5A 6W4

---

## Harlequin  Omnibus

Please check Volumes requested:

- ☐ Essie Summers 1
- ☐ Jean S. MacLeod
- ☐ Eleanor Farnes
- ☐ Susan Barrie
- ☐ Violet Winspear 1
- ☐ Isobel Chace
- ☐ Joyce Dingwell 1
- ☐ Jane Arbor
- ☐ Anne Weale

- ☐ Essie Summers 2
- ☐ Catherine Airlie
- ☐ Mary Burchell 1
- ☐ Sara Seale
- ☐ Violet Winspear 2
- ☐ Rosalind Brett
- ☐ Kathryn Blair
- ☐ Iris Danbury
- ☐ Mary Burchell 2

- ☐ Amanda Doyle
- ☐ Rose Burghley
- ☐ Elizabeth Hoy
- ☐ Roumelia Lane
- ☐ Margaret Malcolm
- ☐ Joyce Dingwell 2
- ☐ Anne Durham
- ☐ Marjorie Norell

Please send me by return mail the books which I have checked.
I am enclosing $1.95 for each book ordered.

Number of books ordered_____ @ $1.95 each = $_____

Postage and Handling = .25

TOTAL $_____

Name _____

Address _____

City _____

State/Prov. _____

Zip/Postal Code _____